Hello, Goodbye

There was a brisk knock at the cabin door. "Who's there?" Emily called out.

"It's me—Chris. That you, Emily? Your folks just got here," he told her. "They're up at the house talking to Mom and Dad."

Emily felt a little funny—both glad and sad. The glad part was because she loved her parents and Eric, and was looking forward to seeing them. The sad part was because they had come to take her home. She hadn't let herself think too much about the end of camp. It meant saying goodbye to all her friends at Webster's—and to Joker. But, on the other hand, it also meant that in just a few days she and Judy would be together again. Then they could start making plans for next summer, when they'd *both* be at Webster's!

Other books in the **HORSE CRAZY** series:

RIDING HOME
by Virginia Vail

Illustrated by Daniel Bodé

Troll Associates

Library of Congress Cataloging-in-Publication Data

Vail, Virginia.
   Riding home / by Virginia Vail; illustrated by Daniel Bode.
     p.   cm.—(Horse crazy; #6)
   Summary: Thirteen-year-old Emily's wonderful summer at Webster's
Country Horse Camp comes to an exciting end, as her cabin acquires a
friendly but exhausting eight-year-old mascot and relatives begin to
gather for Parents' Night.
   ISBN 0-8167-1661-7 (lib. bdg.)   ISBN 0-8167-1662-5 (pbk.)
   [1. Camps—Fiction. 2. Horses—Fiction.] I. Bode, Daniel, ill.
II. Title.   III. Series: Vail, Virginia. Horse crazy; #6.
PZ7.V192Ri   1990
[Fic]—dc20   89-34548

A TROLL BOOK, published by Troll Associates,
Mahwah, NJ 07430

Printed in the United States of America.
10 9 8 7 6 5 4 3 2 1

Riding Home

Chapter One

"All right, Emily. Your turn. Nice and easy," Pam Webster called from the center of the Intermediate riding ring. Danny Franciscus, who had just taken her mount, Misty, over the last jump, slowed the mare to a walk.

Emily Jordan gathered the big palomino's reins and spoke softly to him. "Let's make it a perfect round, Joker. I know you can do it as long as I don't give you the wrong signals, and I'll try not to!" She urged the horse forward with a gentle nudge of her heels, trying to remember everything she'd learned during the past five weeks at Webster's Country Horse Camp. Joker began to canter, and Emily looked straight between his ears, focusing on the first of the five jumps that had been set up in the ring. It was a single bar, two feet off the ground. *No problem,* Emily thought confidently. Joker could fly over something like that in his sleep. The next one, a double-barred gate about a foot higher than the first, should be easy, too. The only jumps Emily was worried about were the low, broad one and the in-and-out. She knew Joker could handle them perfectly unless she fouled up by either slowing him down or making him go too fast. Emily knew timing was very important, particularly when she approached the in-and-out, two jumps placed very close together so Joker wouldn't have much time to prepare for the second one. So far this morning, Emily had taken Joker over the course three times, and every single time they had knocked down the top bar on the very last jump. It wasn't Joker's fault—it was Emily's, and this time she was determined to do everything right for a change. There would be only four more lessons before the final horse show of the season, and Emily wanted more than anything in the world to win a blue ribbon for Joker's sake.

They sailed over the first three jumps with inches to spare. Now they were heading for the in-and-out.

"Easy, boy, easy," Emily whispered to her horse. "I know how much you love to jump, but if we rush it, we'll blow it."

As if he had understood her words, Joker responded immediately to the soft but steady pressure Emily exerted on his mouth, slowing his pace ever so slightly. He cleared the first of the twin jumps, and Emily knew he only had room for two beats of the canter before springing over the second. It would be a perfect round, Emily was certain. She and Joker were on the same wavelength; nothing could possibly go wrong now—

"Hey, Emily, look! See what Daddy bought me? A riding hat just like yours!"

Even if Emily hadn't seen her, she would have recognized little Laura Frick's shrill voice. But she *did* see Laura, who had climbed to the top rail of the fence surrounding the ring and was straddling it, waving her brand new hat high above her head. Joker saw her, too.

Laura's sudden movement threw him off stride for just a fraction of a second. That was all it took to break his rhythm, and there was nothing Emily could do to help. Joker knocked down the top bar for the fourth time that morning, and Emily said between clenched teeth, "Oh, *rats*!" If Laura had been within reach, Emily thought, she would cheerfully have strangled the little girl.

"Sorry, Joker," she sighed, leaning down to pat his silky neck. "We did our best. If it hadn't been for Laura . . ."

"Don't worry about it, Emily," Penny Marshall said as Emily and Joker came up beside her and her mount, Pepper. "You were doing fine until Laura started waving her hat. I guess she doesn't understand how something like that can spook a horse."

Emily nodded. "I know. But it would have been a perfect round, I'm sure of it. I feel bad for Joker—he's embarrassed about fouling up again, I can tell."

Joker snorted and nodded his head vigorously, and Penny giggled. "He's amazing! I think he really *does* know what you're saying."

"Of course he does. Joker's the smartest horse I ever met," Emily said fondly.

4

Just then, Danny trotted up on Misty, her black mare. Like Emily and Penny, she was a Filly—one of the twelve- to fourteen-year-old campers at Webster's—and an intermediate rider. Caro Lescaux, Libby Dexter, and Lynda Graves—also Fillies—were in the Advanced class, and Dru Carpenter, the youngest Filly, was a beginner, so none of them had seen what had happened. "If Laura's coming to the horse show on Sunday, somebody better tie her to the bleachers," Danny said, frowning. "If she does anything like that again, some rider could really get hurt."

"Oh, she'll be coming, all right," Emily said. "She wouldn't miss it. She's going to be around all week, remember, because Libby and I promised Mr. Frick we'd give her a riding lesson every day."

"I think you'd better give her *watching* lessons, too," Penny muttered. "If Laura's going to be a Foal next summer, she has to learn how to act around horses."

As the last horse and rider completed the course, Pam shouted, "Okay, girls, that's it for today. Take your horses back to the stables and cool them down. I'll see you at lunch . . . ." Her voice trailed off. Laura had just jumped into the ring from her perch on the fence and was heading toward Emily, Penny, and Danny, brown eyes shining below her thick, smooth bangs. The eight-year-old reminded Emily of a plump little squirrel, all bright-eyed and bushy-tailed, as Libby's grandmother would say. Before she reached the girls, Pam strode over to her and touched her on the shoulder. "Laura, slow down!"

she commanded. "I think we have to have a little talk."

"Sure!" Laura beamed up at her. "What do you want to talk about, Pam?"

Penny and Danny started to follow the other riders out of the ring, but Emily decided to wait. After all, Laura was kind of her responsibility, since it was because of Emily that she was there at all.

Laura's father had first shown up at Webster's last week. None of the campers knew he was planning on becoming Matt's partner—in fact, Emily and the rest of the Fillies were sure he wanted to buy the property and turn it into a vacation resort. With the help of the others, Emily tried to convince him that Webster's was a terrible place where no one would want to spend a vacation. When Mr. Frick found out he had been tricked, he was very angry, but he promised to forgive and forget if Emily and Libby would give his little daughter riding lessons. It seemed like a fair trade to Emily, but she hadn't realized at the time what she was letting herself in for.

Now Pam was saying to Laura, "If you're going to be spending the rest of the week here, Laura, you have to learn to behave properly around horses. We have certain rules here at Webster's—"

"I know," Laura cheerfully chirped. "Always wear a hard hat when you ride and always cool your horse down after you ride, and clean out your horse's stall, and . . ."

"Whoa!" Pam held up a hand like a traffic cop. "Those rules are very important, but there's another one that's important, too, and that is, *never* do anything to scare a horse when somebody's riding him. He might shy, and his rider could be thrown. It's just lucky that Joker has plenty of horse sense or Emily might have been hurt this morning."

Laura's eyes widened. "Oh, you mean when I waved at her? Gee, Pam, I didn't mean to scare Joker. I'd feel just *awful* if Emily got hurt! Or Libby. They're my friends, and they're teaching me how to ride, so, if they got hurt, somebody else would have to teach me, I guess. Do you think maybe I'll be able to ride in the horse show on Sunday if I learn real fast? They're giving me another lesson this afternoon. Want to watch? Maybe you could teach me, too!"

"Laura, just remember what I said, okay? Don't scare the horses." Pam glanced at her watch. "Lunch will be ready in about half an hour. Do you want to come up to the farmhouse with me now?"

Laura shook her head. "Oh, no! I want to go back to the stable with Emily and say hello to Cupcake. I'm pretending he's my pony because he's the one I rode yesterday and the day before. I don't want him to forget me. I brought some sugar lumps for him from home. He won't get cavities or anything if I give him sugar, will he?"

"I don't imagine a couple of sugar lumps will do him any harm," Pam said. "See you later, Laura." She walked off, pausing beside Emily and Joker to say, "You handled Joker beautifully, Emily. I think Laura understands now why she shouldn't be so rambunctious around horses."

"Thanks, Pam." Emily smiled gratefully at the older girl.

Pam gave Joker a pat. "Here comes your prize pupil now. I'm going to disappear before she asks me any more questions!"

Laura trotted over then and looked up at Emily, her round face solemn. "I'm sorry about scaring Joker, Emily. I didn't mean to, honest! I just wanted to show you my new hat. Daddy bought me new boots, too. See?" She stuck out one foot for Emily's inspection. "They're just like yours, too! I didn't know horses got scared of people. They're so big, I didn't think they were scared of anything! Hey, Emily, you're not mad at me, are you? I think Pam is. Pam's awful bossy, isn't she?"

"I'm not mad at you," Emily said, "and neither is Pam. And she's not really bossy. She just wants to teach you how to act around horses, the way she's been teaching all of us."

"Well, *I* think she's bossy. Are you taking Joker back to the stable now?"

Emily nodded. "I have to take off his saddle and bridle and make sure he's comfortable before I have lunch."

"Hey, Emily, will you let me ride Joker some time?" Laura asked, stroking Joker's nose. "He's the most beautiful horse at Webster's! He's even more beautiful than Cupcake. Could I ride him back to the stable? You could lead him, and I'd just sit on him. *Please*, Emily?"

"Well . . ." Emily hesitated, then said, "Sure—why not?" She dismounted and showed Laura how

to put one foot in her linked hands so she could lift her into the saddle.

"Wow!" Laura grabbed the reins, and her face lit up with a big grin. "It's like sitting on a *mountain*! I'm so *high*!"

Emily couldn't help smiling as she led the big palomino out of the ring with Laura on his back. And her smile broadened as Laura said, "You know something, Emily? You're the nicest person I've met at Webster's. It's kind of like you're my big sister or something. I don't have any sisters or brothers— there's only me. I always wanted to have a big sister, only it's too late now, I guess. Do you have a little sister?"

"Nope," Emily said. "In my family, I'm the little sister. My brother Eric is two years older than me."

"Then can I be your little sister?" Laura asked eagerly. "My best friend Sandy is at camp for two weeks, and there's an older girl there who's her big sister. She isn't really—just at camp. But Sandy's camp isn't like Webster's. They don't even have horses! Isn't that awful? I wouldn't want to go to a camp like that, would you? I know I'm not really a camper, but I will be next summer. I'm going to be a Foal, and you'll still be a Filly, won't you? So you could be my big sister next year, too!"

"I'll think about it," Emily promised. What she was really thinking about was how much Laura had to say, and how fast she said it!

As they came into the stable yard, Libby waved at Emily. "What kept you?" she said. "And why is Laura riding Joker?" Libby had taken off her riding hat, and her mop of unruly red curls caught the midday sunshine. "I bet I know! From now on, Joker's going to be Laura's horse, and you're going to be riding Cupcake, right?"

"Very funny!" Emily pretended to scowl at Libby. "Joker's *my* horse. Laura wanted to ride him back to the stable, so I said it was okay."

"And Emily's going to be my big sister!" Laura sang out. "But I could have *two* big sisters, Libby. Wanna be the other one?"

"I'll think about it," Libby said, echoing Emily's words. "Hurry up, Emily, or you're going to be late for lunch. Want to come with me, Laura? You can sit with the Foals if you get there in time."

"Oh, no!" Laura said. "I want to sit with the Fillies."

"I thought you'd want to get to know some girls your own age," Libby said. "There are a lot of eight-year-old Foals."

Laura's face fell. "Don't you want me to sit with you?" she quavered, and her lower lip trembled. "You and Emily are my best friends at Webster's. Don't you like me anymore?"

"Of course we like you," Emily quickly assured her. "I told you the other day you could be our mascot, remember? You don't have to sit with the Foals if you don't want to."

Laura beamed. "I'm glad! I'll get to know the Foals later. 'Bye, Libby. I'm going to help Emily unsaddle Joker now, and then I'm going to give Cupcake some sugar lumps, and then Emily and I will

11

come up to the farmhouse for lunch. At the Fillies' table."

As Libby waved and sprinted off, Emily said, "If you're going to help me take care of Joker, first you have to get off. We can't unsaddle him while you're still sitting on his back."

"No, we can't, can we? You don't have to help me—I can get off all by myself." And Laura did, landing beside Emily with a thump. "Can I lead him into the stable? I know where he lives. Can I give him one of my sugar lumps? Does he like sugar? What does Joker like to eat best? How old is he? Who's his best friend? His best *horse* friend, I mean. I guess you're his best people friend. Do horses have best friends? I bet they do. Maybe Caro's horse Vic is Joker's best friend since they're next-door neighbors. Vic's nice but he's not as nice as Joker. Caro's pretty, isn't she? Do you think I'm going to be pretty when I get old like Caro?"

The questions came so fast that Emily didn't bother to answer. She just let Laura chatter away while they went into the stable. Then she showed her how to unbuckle Joker's girth and undo the throat latch of his bridle—Emily took them off because Laura couldn't reach that high. As they rubbed Joker down, Laura said, "Now that Daddy's going to be Mr. Webster's partner, it's kind of like all the horses half belong to him, isn't it? And if they half belong to him, they belong to me a quarter, don't they? I like math. Do you like math? Are we done now? Can I give the rest of my sugar lumps to Cupcake?"

12

Emily waited patiently while Laura visited Cupcake in his stall. When the pony had polished off the last sugar lump, Laura came skipping back and slipped her sticky little hand into Emily's. "Come on, Emily," she said. "Let's eat real fast so you and Libby can give me my riding lesson."

"We're going to give you your lesson a little later," Emily told her. "First there's water sports down at the river."

"Oh, good! I love to swim! I brought my bathing suit just in case. Can I swim with you and Libby and the rest of the Fillies? Oh, boy! I just *love* being at Webster's! Hurry up, Emily, or else there won't be anything left to eat!"

Chapter Two

For the rest of the day, Laura never let Emily out of her sight except when she was tagging along after Libby. At lunch she sat between them, wolfing down a surprising amount of food for such a little girl and managing to keep up a steady stream of conversation at the same time. When Libby suggested that she might like to take a nap during rest period while the Fillies wrote letters home, sunbathed, or read, Laura shook her head vigorously.

"Oh, no. I'm not sleepy at all. I stopped taking naps *ages* ago! What are you going to do, Emily?"

"I'm going to write to my friend Judy," Emily told her.

"Your very best friend, the one who broke her leg and couldn't come to camp with you?"

Emily nodded.

"Can I write to her, too?" Laura asked eagerly. "I write very good script." She peered over Emily's shoulder as Emily took out her pad of Webster's Country Horse Camp stationery with the little green

14

figure of a horse on it. "Oh, that's neat! Can I use some of your paper? I'll write a letter to your friend Judy and you can stick it in the same envelope with yours. And then I'll write a letter to *my* best friend, Sandy. Libby, do you have a pen I can borrow?"

After rest period, the Fillies all trooped down to the dock for water sports, and Laura skipped along at Emily's side, still talking a mile a minute.

"Did you know that Daddy's going to build a great big swimming pool so we don't have to swim in the river all the time? It's going to be neat, with diving boards and everything! And he's going to build a tennis court, too. Do you know how to play tennis? I don't, but I'm going to learn. Daddy's going to buy me a racket and lots of balls. I like the colored ones—yellow, green, and orange. He's going to buy me some cute tennis outfits, too. Melinda's the swimming teacher, isn't she? I think she's real pretty. But Caro's prettier."

Caro smiled at her, obviously pleased by the compliment.

"Melinda's Warren Webster's girlfriend, isn't she?" Laura went on. "Do you have a boyfriend, Caro? I bet you do. Is he as handsome as Warren?"

"*More* handsome," Caro said, catching Emily's eye. "He's Emily's brother."

"Emily's brother is your boyfriend? Oh, wow! That's really neat! Who's *your* boyfriend, Emily?"

Emily rolled her eyes. "I don't have a boyfriend," she said. "I like horses better than boys!"

"Me, too!" Laura grinned at her. "I guess Cup-

15

cake's *my* boyfriend. He's the cutest pony I ever saw."

By the time Emily and Libby had given Laura her riding lesson and Mr. Frick had persuaded his protesting daughter that it really was time to go home, Emily's ears were ringing with the echoes of Laura's constant chatter. She waved until Mr. Frick's little red car was out of sight, then heaved a huge sigh.

"Are all little sisters like that?" she asked Lynda as they trudged back to the Fillies' bunkhouse to wash up for supper.

Lynda shrugged. "Search me. I only have little brothers. But Laura's something else, all right. She's a nice kid, though."

"I think she's lonely," Danny added, catching up to Lynda and Emily. "I'd be lonely if I was an only child. I guess we're going to be seeing a lot of Laura until the camp season ends on Sunday."

Emily pushed open the screen door to the cabin and flung herself onto her bunk, hoping to get a few minutes' rest before the evening meal. She had hardly closed her eyes when Libby's red curly head hung down from the bunk above.

"How about taking turns with Laura's lessons?" she asked. "You do it tomorrow, and I'll do it on Wednesday, okay?"

Instead of answering directly, Emily said, " 'I have a little shadow that goes in and out with me . . .' "

" ' . . . and what can be the use of him'—or in this case, *her*— 'is more than I can see,' " Libby finished.

Emily giggled. "You got it! Okay, Libby, you're on. I wonder when she'll show up tomorrow? Ever since Mr. Frick became Matt's partner, they've been getting here earlier and earlier! I wonder how Laura's mother feels about her spending so much time at Webster's."

"She's probably happy because she knows how much Laura's enjoying it," Penny said. "Don't you think so, Dru?"

Dru didn't say anything. She just nodded. Emily thought she looked sad, the way she used to when she first arrived at Webster's. She hadn't looked that way in a long time.

"Dru?" Emily frowned. "Is something wrong?"

Dru sighed. "No . . . not really . . . ."

"Do you think the Websters will let Laura be in the horse show?" Danny asked. "She said she'd asked Pam, and Pam didn't say she couldn't. But she didn't say she could, either."

"Since she's not an official camper, I don't think she should be allowed to compete," Lynda said. "But maybe she could ride Cupcake in the final parade. That would make her folks happy. All the parents will be there for the show—except mine, of course. They can't come all the way from Iowa."

"My family's coming," Danny said. "They wouldn't miss it for anything!"

"Neither would Gram and Grandpa," Libby added. "They're coming Saturday morning and taking me home after the show on Sunday."

"My mother and father are coming, too," Caro said.

"So are mine," said Emily. "And so is Eric. Judy wanted to, but she's going on vacation with her parents. Parents' Weekend is going to be super!"

Dru stood up. "I have to go to the bathroom," she said.

"Wait a minute, Dru." Caro placed herself in Dru's path so the younger girl had to come face to face with her. "Something *is* wrong," Caro said. "Want to tell us about it?"

"No." Dru stared down at the floor, keeping her lips tightly closed over her braces. "Are you going to let me go to the bathroom?"

Caro made an elaborate bow. "Be my guest," she said, and Dru went into the bathroom, closing the door behind her.

Caro sighed. "Honestly! I thought she'd gotten over being so gloomy. Do *you* know what's wrong, Penny? You're Dru's best friend."

Penny shook her head. "She hasn't said anything. Maybe she's just sad because this is the last week of camp. She didn't like Webster's at first, but she loves it now. And she loves Donna, too. She's going to miss that little mare a lot, I bet."

Emily could understand that because she knew how much she was going to miss Joker. And yet she had a feeling that something else was bothering Dru.

"Well, it's silly for her to get all bent out of shape about that now, while she's still here," Caro said. "And we all have a lot of things to think about besides Dru. The Foals, the Fillies, and the Thoros are all supposed to come up with skits for Saturday

18

night when all the parents are here, and we don't have a clue about what we're going to do."

"Oh, wow! You're right, Caro," Libby said. "We have to come up with something fast."

"And then there's the video," Lynda put in.

The rest of the Fillies stared at her. "What video?" Danny asked. "What're you talking about?"

"You know—the video Warren's going to shoot of all of us doing our thing at Webster's so Matt and Marie can send it to girls who are thinking of coming here next summer." She looked around at five blank faces. "Hey, didn't any of you see the notice on the bulletin board by the camp store? Matt put it up today right after lunch."

"A video? Of all of us? How did I miss it?" Caro wondered aloud. "When is Warren going to do it? Is he going to film all the classes, and the trail rides, and even the horse show? Will we be able to order tapes for ourselves? What a neat idea!"

"I didn't see the notice, either," Emily said. "But then I've been pretty busy with Laura."

"So have I," Libby said. "I didn't know Warren had a video camera."

"Maybe he rented one," Danny suggested. "My dad did that once or twice. It's really fun to see yourself on TV, kind of like being a movie star or something."

All the Fillies were talking excitedly about the video when the bathroom door opened and Dru came out.

"Hey, Dru, guess what?" Penny cried. "We're going to make a video!"

Dru nodded. "I know. I saw the notice on the bulletin board."

"Just think—it'll be like having our horses with us all year long," Emily said. "Whenever we get lonely for them, we can just play the tape and there they'll be. Won't that be terrific?" The thought of having Joker available any time she turned on the VCR was so wonderful that she couldn't imagine why she hadn't thought to ask her father to rent a camcorder on his last visit.

"Yeah—terrific," Dru said with a sigh.

But her lack of enthusiasm didn't dampen anyone else's spirits. They were still talking about it when they heard the clang of the big dinner bell calling them to supper. Pam was already seated at the Fillies' table when they trooped into the dining room of the farmhouse, and everyone immediately bombarded her with questions. As soon as she could get a word in edgewise, Pam said, "Cool out, girls! Dad's going to explain everything right after supper. In the meantime, has anybody thought about what you're going to do for Parents' Night?"

"We're writing a skit—it's almost done, and it's going to be really funny," Janet, one of the Thoros, said as she put a big bowl of fragrant, steaming stew in the middle of the table. The Thoros were serving this evening, and the Fillies were on clean-up detail. "And don't ask me to tell you what it's about. You'll find out Saturday night."

"I guess we'd better think of something fast," Lynda said.

"What are the Foals going to do?" Danny asked.

"Melinda says they're preparing a talent show," Pam replied. "One of them tap-dances, another one does gymnastics, and I think some of the others are forming a rhythm band. There's a baton twirler, too, and a girl who plays the violin."

"I could do a dramatic reading," Danny suggested hopefully. "Maybe a chapter from *National Velvet*?" Everybody groaned. They all knew that Danny had read the book at least fourteen times. "Well, it was just a thought." Danny helped herself to a plate of stew and began eating, the picture of injured dignity.

"That's an interesting idea, Danny," Pam said, ladling stew onto the other girls' plates, "but I think we need to come up with something a little zingier, if you know what I mean."

"You know," Libby mused aloud, "my grandpa sings with a barbershop quartet. They do real old-fashioned music, and some of it's pretty corny, but it's funny, too. They really ham it up."

"Hey, that's not a bad idea," Lynda said. "Maybe we could do a Gay Nineties bit, with big fake mustaches and those round straw hats men used to wear . . ."

"And we could make up silly words to old songs," Caro added. "That would be fun!"

"But there are only four people in a quartet, and there are seven of us," Penny pointed out.

Even Dru was beginning to brighten up. "Is there such a thing as a *seventet*?" she asked, and the other girls laughed.

"Maybe there didn't used to be, but I don't see why we can't have one."

Pam smiled at her young charges. "I think you're on to something, Fillies. Why don't you get together tonight after cleanup and work out the details? I'll help you any way I can."

The girls chattered happily as they finished their supper, so absorbed in their plans for Parents' Night that they completely forgot about the video. It wasn't until they were finishing the delicious peach cobbler Marie had made for dessert and Matt stood up to make an announcement that they were reminded of it.

When he had gotten everyone's attention, Matt said, "I guess by now all of you have seen the notice I put up today about the video we're going to be making over the next few days here at Webster's."

The girls all murmured and nodded enthusiastically.

"This is a first for the camp," Matt went on, "and we're very excited about it, as I'm sure you are. The video camera that Warren will be using to shoot the video was a gift from my new partner, Mr. Larry Frick . . . ."

"Oh, wow!" Libby whispered to Emily. "Good thing we didn't manage to scare him away!" Emily grinned and nodded.

" . . . so, even though he's not here tonight, I think we ought to give him a big hand."

Matt began to clap, and all the campers joined him, whistling and cheering. Rachel and the Thoros began to sing:

"For he's a jolly good fellow,
For he's a jolly good fellow!
For he's a jolly good fellow,
Which nobody can deny!"

The rest of the campers and counselors joined in:

"Which nobody can deny,
Which nobody can deny!
For he's a jolly good fellow,
Which nobody can deny!"

Laughing, Matt said, "Too bad Warren wasn't here to tape that tribute. But, if you happen to run into Mr. Frick, it would be nice if you thanked him personally. I know he'd appreciate it. Now to get down to details. Warren's going to be covering all the camp activities, starting tomorrow morning, so don't be surprised if you see him with the camcorder leaning over your shoulder when you're grooming your horses, taking your riding classes, or doing anything else you normally do at Webster's. He took a course last year at school on videotaping and editing, so he knows what he's doing—or so he tells me!"

Everyone laughed.

Meghan, a Thoro, raised her hand, and when Matt nodded to her, she said, "Is Warren going to cover Parents' Night and the horse show on Sunday?"

"Yep—everything we do at Webster's from now on, so girls who are considering coming to our camp next summer will be able to see exactly what they have to look forward to."

Caro waved her hand wildly. "Can we order copies of the tape?" she asked.

"You sure can. We'll try to keep the cost as low as possible, so every camper can see herself in living color."

A Foal piped up, "What about the food? Marie's meals are so fantastic that everybody ought to see how good they are."

Marie, who had come out of the kitchen to listen to the announcement, smiled and blushed.

Matt grinned. "Yes, the food, too. We want to show every prospective camper all the good things about Webster's, and one of the *best* things is Marie's terrific meals. I ought to know—I have the privilege of eating them all year round. Believe it or not, my wife doesn't stop cooking after you all leave!" He looked around the dining room. "Any other questions?"

There were a few, and Matt answered them, then told everyone to finish their desserts so the Fillies could clear their plates. He sat down to a spatter of applause, and Emily finished the last of her peach cobbler. As far as she was concerned, Joker ought to be the star of the video because he was the most beautiful horse at Webster's. She could hardly wait until Warren started taping tomorrow morning!

Chapter Three

When Emily returned to the Fillies' cabin the next morning after her usual early visit to Joker in the pasture where the horses spent the night, she found everybody wide awake for a change—even Caro, who was always the last to roll out of bed. Caro's bunk was hidden beneath a huge pile of clothes, and she was rummaging through them, still in her underwear.

"I don't have a *thing* to wear!" she moaned, and all the other Fillies whooped with laughter.

Pam, who was already dressed in jeans, boots, and a plaid shirt, grinned at her. "Caro, you have more clothes than all the other campers put together! Just close your eyes and pick something out—*anything*. The idea is for everybody to look natural, as though this was a normal day at Webster's."

"I think we all ought to wear our Webster's T-shirts," Danny said, fastening her thick, dark hair back with a rubber band. She had on a white shirt with "Webster's Country Horse Camp" printed across the chest in green.

Emily agreed. She was wearing her Webster's T-shirt, too. "Come on, Caro—hurry up. We're supposed to set up for breakfast, you know, and we don't want to be late."

"Oh, all right," Caro sighed, and started getting dressed. "You all go ahead. I'll meet you at the farmhouse after I put on some makeup."

Emily paused on her way out the door. "Don't overdo it," she advised. "Eric will be seeing the video, and like he told you, he doesn't think girls look good with a lot of gook on their faces."

"I am *not* going to put on a lot of gook," Caro said, peering at herself in the mirror over the bureau. "Just a little eye makeup so I don't look like a white rabbit. Sometimes I wish I wasn't so blond. Then you could see that I actually have eyebrows and eyelashes!"

"Just make it snappy," Pam told her. "We have a busy day ahead of us."

As the Fillies came into the kitchen a few minutes later, they discovered that Warren was already there with the camcorder, taping Marie while she took a tin of freshly baked golden-brown muffins out of the oven.

"Better do it again, Mom," he said. "And try to stand a little to the side this time so we can see the muffins instead of your rear end."

"Warren, dear, this is the *third time*," Marie said, sliding the muffins back into the oven. "At this rate,

I'll have to start preparing lunch before breakfast is over!"

"Just once more, I promise. Okay—on your mark, get set, *go!*"

This time, Warren was satisfied, much to Marie's relief. "You just go about your business the way you normally would," she told the Fillies. "Try to pretend Warren's not here. You'll get used to him after a while—Warren honey, could you kind of step over there, next to the sink? The girls have to get to the dining room to set the tables, and you're blocking the door."

Warren sighed. "Mom, if this tape's going to be any good at all, I have to have freedom of movement. You can't just shove me in a corner and expect me to capture everything that's going on," he protested. "Libby, quit making faces, okay? Act *natural.*"

"She *is* acting natural," Lynda giggled.

Caro frowned at both girls. "There's such a thing as being *too* natural." Then she smiled at Warren. "When I'm on camera, try to remember that my right side is my best side. My nose looks funny from the left."

"Believe me, Caro, nobody's going to notice your nose," Warren said between clenched teeth. "Just do your thing and try to forget I'm here, like Mom says."

Emily picked up a tray of dishes and headed for the dining room door. "Come on, Caro, take the other tray and let's set the tables," she said.

"Coming," Caro sang out sweetly. She picked up

the second tray and followed Emily, keeping the right side of her face turned to Warren and the camera.

"Caro, look out!" Danny yelled, but it was too late. Because she wasn't looking where she was going, Caro walked right into the doorframe, and cups, saucers, and plates went flying.

"Oh, no!" Marie groaned as Penny and Dru ran over and started picking up the pieces.

Caro blushed bright red. "Gee, Marie, I'm awfully sorry," she muttered, then glanced at Warren. "I guess I ruined that shot, huh?"

"You would have if I'd had the thing turned on," he growled. "Fortunately, I didn't. Maybe I better forget about taping breakfast. The way things are going, maybe we ought to forget about breakfast, period!"

"Don't be silly, dear," Marie said briskly. "Everybody has to eat. Caro, don't worry about the dishes—we have plenty more. Lynda, why don't you start beating these eggs? Libby, you and Danny set out the boxes of cereal. Dru, please start pouring the milk. Penny and Caro, get some more dishes and help Emily finish setting the tables. The rest of the campers will be here any minute now. Warren, I think you should take the camera into the dining room so you can tape the girls as they come in and take their places."

Once order was restored, the preparations for breakfast proceeded quickly and efficiently. Warren stationed himself in a corner of the dining room and began taping again as the Thoros and Foals trooped in, laughing and chattering. After the Fillies had finished serving, they joined Pam at their table.

"You missed all the excitement, Pam," Emily said, digging into her scrambled eggs. "Warren started taping while we were fixing breakfast, and it was wild!"

Pam grinned. "I had to talk to Dad about a couple of things, but I was planning on lending you guys a hand—until I heard the crash. Then I changed my mind. What happened, anyway?"

Everybody had just started to tell her, when Emily heard a familiar, piping voice.

"Hey, Emily, is there room for me at your table? I already had breakfast, but I'd just love one of those muffins! What kind are they? Blueberry? Oh, great! I *love* blueberry muffins!"

Laura Frick wriggled into the empty chair next to Emily, her round, rosy face wreathed in smiles, and reached for the last muffin in the basket.

"Is there any butter left? Is that honey in that pot? I *love* honey on my muffins. Can I have a glass of milk? Thanks, Pam. Oh, Warren's started taping already!" She bounced up and down, waving at Warren. "Hi, Warren! Isn't that camera neat? It's just like ours at home. Daddy tapes absolutely *everything*! But he didn't tell me he was buying one for Webster's until this morning—he wanted it to be a surprise, and I guess he was afraid I couldn't keep a secret. I guess he was right. I'm just *terrible* at keeping secrets!" Laura took a big bite out of her muffin. "Mmmm, delicious! Guess what, Libby—Daddy says that with the horse show coming up on Sunday,

31

he's going to let me have *two* riding lessons every day instead of one. Isn't that neat? Emily can give me one and you can give me the other. That's so I'll get real good by Sunday. My mom can't wait to see me ride in the horse show."

Emily looked at Libby, and then they both looked at Pam. Pam looked at Laura. "Gee, Laura," she said, "I don't know if Libby and Emily are going to have time to give you two lessons a day. They have a lot of other things to do, you know, like working up their act with the other Fillies for Parents' Night."

"Yeah, we have a lot of practicing to do," Libby said.

Laura's smile faded and her voice started shaking as she said, "But Daddy *said* . . ."

Pam smiled at her, but Emily thought her smile was a little strained. "I think we ought to check with my father about your competing in the horse show. It's really just for registered campers, you know."

"Oh, I know that's the way it *used* to be," Laura chirped. "But that was before Daddy became Mr. Webster's partner. He's talking to Mr. Webster right now. I'm sure it will be all right. Because my mom really wants to see me riding on Sunday. I've told her all about Cupcake!" She glanced at Emily's plate. "If you're not going to eat all your bacon and eggs, I'll finish them for you. I just *love* bacon and eggs!"

"Be my guest," Emily sighed, pushing her plate in front of Laura, and Laura began cheerfully gobbling up the remains of her breakfast.

Just then, Melinda came over to the Fillies' table. She was holding the hand of one of the Foals, a freckle-faced little girl named Jennifer who was around Laura's age.

"Hi, Laura," Melinda said. "Remember me?"

"Sure." Laura smiled at her. "You're a really good swimmer. And you're Warren's girlfriend, too."

Melinda blushed. "Uh . . . yes, I guess I am. I'm also the Foals' counselor. And this is Jennifer."

Jennifer grinned shyly. "Hi, Laura."

"Hi," Laura said, taking another forkful of scrambled eggs.

"I thought maybe you'd like to take riding class with Jennifer and the rest of the beginners this morning," Melinda went on. "Rachel said it would be okay—she's the beginning riding instructor."

Laura nodded. "I know. Thank you very much, Melinda, but I'm having *private* lessons with Emily and Libby."

"Yes, but wouldn't it be more fun with a group of girls your own age?" Melinda asked.

"Yeah, Laura. We have *lots* of fun," Jennifer added. "And I can introduce you to the other Foals. You could even sit at our table for lunch."

"Oh, no," Laura said quickly. "The Fillies are my friends, and Libby and Emily are my big sisters. Besides, Daddy wants me to have private lessons so I can make up for lost time. Thanks, anyway."

"Well, if you change your mind . . ." Melinda said.

33

Laura polished off the rest of Emily's breakfast. "I won't."

Jennifer scowled and tugged at Melinda's hand. "I told you she wouldn't," she whispered, but it was a loud enough whisper so that Emily could hear, and Laura could, too. "She's stuck up because her father's Matt's new partner. Who needs her?"

"Jennifer!" Melinda frowned at the little girl, then glanced across the table at Pam and shrugged. "Well, I tried."

They marched back to the Foals' table, and Laura stared down at her empty plate. "That wasn't very nice, what Jennifer said," she mumbled. "I am *not* stuck up!"

"Of course you're not," Danny said kindly. "I bet Jennifer would change her mind if she got to know you."

Laura shook her head. "No, she wouldn't. She doesn't like me and I don't like *her* and I don't want to be friends with her, so there!"

Libby pushed her chair back from the table and stood up. "Guess we'd better make tracks for the stable. Coming, Emily?"

Before Emily could reply, Laura jumped up. "I'll come with you, Libby! I brought lots of carrots for Cupcake and Foxy and Joker. In one of my horse books it says that carrots and apples and stuff are better for horses than sugar lumps. I'll help you groom Foxy and then you can help me with Cupcake, okay?"

She trotted off at Libby's side, followed by Caro,

Danny, and Penny. Lynda, Emily, and Dru lingered behind.

"Pam, do you think Matt is going to let Laura ride in the show?" Lynda asked. "If he does, it really wouldn't be fair, you know."

Pam shrugged. "Search me. Dad may make an exception in her case if Mr. Frick insists. But I agree—it wouldn't be fair to all the other girls who have been here all season. It's not up to me, though. We'll just have to see."

"Do Libby and I have to give her two riding lessons?" Emily asked. "If we do, that'll tie us up for most of the afternoon, and we *do* need to practice for Parents' Night."

"I know. That's why I asked Melinda to try to get her to join the beginners' class," Pam said. "I'll go talk to Dad and see what he has to say." She headed for Matt's office, calling over her shoulder, "See you later."

Dru continued to sit at the table, looking glum.

"Dru? You coming?" Emily said.

Dru heaved a sigh. "I guess so." But she didn't budge.

Emily met Lynda's eyes, and the two of them each took a chair on either side of Dru.

"Okay, Dru, what is it? What's wrong?" Lynda said, plunking her elbows on the table and resting her chin in her hands.

"You might as well tell us," Emily added. "Why are you so sad all of a sudden? You've been doing so well, and you're not scared of horses anymore or anything. Is it because you're going to miss Donna when the season's over? I'm going to miss Joker, too, but it won't be so bad now that I know I'll have him on videotape whenever I get lonely for him."

"It's not that." Dru stared down at her empty plate. "It's just . . ."

"Just *what*?" Lynda said. "We're your friends. You can tell us."

"Oh, all right." Dru raised her head and looked from Lynda to Emily. "It's my folks. Remember I told you they're getting a divorce?"

Emily and Lynda nodded.

"Well, I tried not to think about it after I started having fun here at Webster's, and I *didn't* think about it until now. But now everybody's parents are coming for the weekend and taking them home, but I don't know who's coming for me, and I don't know what home I'm going to! What if neither of them comes? Or what if *both* of them come and they have a big fight or something? Either way, it's going to be awful."

Neither Emily nor Lynda could think of anything to say. Dru had a problem, all right, and there wasn't an easy solution. As one of the Foals cleared their table, the three girls sat in silence. Finally Lynda said, "Hey, Dru, they're not going to just *leave* you here. They're probably figuring out which one of them gets first dibs on you, know what I mean? One of them is sure to show up. Don't worry about it. None of my family is going to be here for Parents' Weekend, and I'm not all bent out of shape."

"That's because you know your folks love you and

36

they'd be here if they could," Dru mumbled. "I'm not sure my folks love me at all."

"Of course they do!" Emily exclaimed. "You're a very lovable person."

Dru blinked at her. "Do you really think so?" she asked hopefully. "Even though I'm not as pretty or athletic as my sisters and brother?"

Emily giggled. "Come on, Dru! Is your brother really pretty?"

Now Dru smiled a little. "You know what I mean."

"We don't *know* your brother and sisters," Lynda pointed out. "We know *you,* and we like you just the way you are. I bet your folks will be real proud when they see how much weight you've lost and what a good rider you are."

"Yes, Dru," Emily added. "And you've made a lot of friends here at Webster's. We've only known you for five weeks, and your parents have known you your entire *life.* Of course they love you."

Dru thought about that for a moment. "Maybe," she said at last. "I guess I'll just have to wait and see what happens when they show up—*if* they show up."

Lynda stood up. "Right. Now there's another friend who's waiting for you—Donna. I bet she's beginning to wonder if you've forgotten all about her."

Dru and Emily got up, too. "Gee, I wouldn't want her to think that," Dru said. "She's a very sensitive mare. I'd hate to hurt her feelings. Come on, Lynda, Emily. Let's go!"

Chapter Four

About half an hour later, Emily had finished spreading fresh, clean straw in Joker's stall and was starting to comb the burrs out of his long, silvery tail. Joker wasn't enjoying it very much.

"I'm sorry, Joker," Emily told him. "I don't want to hurt you, but your tail really is a mess, you know, and you have to look your best for the videotape."

"Can I borrow the comb when you're through?" Caro asked from the stall next door. "Vic got into the burrs, too."

"Sure. I'll be finished in a minute," Emily said.

"Uh . . . Emily, when is your family arriving for Parents' Weekend?" Caro said casually, leaning on the partition that separated the two stalls.

Emily grinned at her. "Do you mean Eric hasn't given you the exact hour of his arrival in one of those letters he keeps sending?"

"Well, he *did* mention something about trying to get here on Friday afternoon. I was just wondering if they were still planning on coming then, because of the moonlight trail ride."

"Oh, yeah—I'd forgotten about that," Emily said. "As far as I know, they'll be here in time for supper, and I bet Eric would just *love* to go on the trail ride."

"Oh, good!" Caro sighed dreamily. "It'll be so romantic, riding side by side along the river in the moonlight. . . ."

"What does it feel like, Caro?" Emily asked suddenly.

"What does what feel like?"

"Being in love." When Caro didn't answer right away, Emily said, "I mean it. I really want to know."

"Well . . . it's kind of hard to describe," Caro murmured. "It's like . . . well, it's feeling happy whenever you think about him, and wanting to be with him all the time, and missing him when he's not there. And when he *is* there, you feel all warm and glowy inside."

"Oh, I get it," Emily said. "Then I *do* know what it feels like. That's exactly the way I feel about Joker!"

Caro rolled her eyes. "Honestly! It's not the same thing at all."

Emily shrugged cheerfully. "Sounds like it to me. Here—I'm finished with the comb."

"Thanks." Caro took it and began working on Vic's tail, humming under her breath.

As Emily brushed Joker's golden coat, she couldn't help thinking how much Caro had changed over the past few weeks. Emily hadn't liked her at all when they had first met—none of the Fillies did,

because Caro acted like such a snob. And when Caro had tried to trick Emily into trading horses with her for the season, Emily got really mad. She'd stood up to Caro rather than giving in as she might once have done. Nobody, not even Princess Caroline, was going to take her beloved Joker away from her, not if she could help it!

I guess I've changed a lot, too, Emily thought, resting her cheek against Joker's silky neck for a moment. *This has been the best summer of my life—and to think, I almost didn't come to Webster's because I was afraid I'd be lonely without Judy!*

"Hi, Emily! Guess what? I cleaned out Cupcake's stall all by myself. And I groomed him and everything!" Laura's head popped up over the door to Joker's stall. "I gave him a carrot, and then I gave one to Foxy and Misty and Tonto."

"Who's Tonto?" Emily asked, putting Joker's saddle pad on his back.

"He's Jennifer's horse," Laura told her. "I saved a nice fat carrot for Joker, too." She held out the carrot and Joker promptly devoured it.

"I thought you didn't like Jennifer," Emily said as she heaved Joker's saddle on top of the pad and began fastening the girth.

"Well, I don't really, but I like her horse. He's Cupcake's next-door neighbor, and he looked so sad when I gave a carrot to Cupcake that I felt sorry for him, so I gave him one. Jennifer said thank you."

"That's nice." Now Emily took off Joker's halter and put on his bridle. "Are you going to watch the riding classes this morning?"

41

"Oh, yes! And I'll be very quiet so I don't scare the horses. And then I'm going to have lunch with the Fillies, and *then* you're going to give me one lesson and Libby's going to give me another one. And Warren's going to make a special tape of my lessons for Daddy and Mommy! Isn't that neat? And after that . . ."

"After that we have to work up our act for Parents' Night," Caro said firmly. She had finished saddling Vic and now she led him out of his stall.

"Oh, good!" Laura chirped happily. "That sounds like fun. What's your act going to be? Can I be in it? I was in my class play last spring—it was *Peter Rabbit* and I was Flopsy. Everybody said I was so good I should have played Peter, but Miss Newman gave the part to Danny Trevino just because he's a boy. I learned all his lines, though, and all the songs. Maybe we could do *Peter Rabbit* for Parents' Night and this time I could be Peter! I can't wait to tell Daddy!" And she dashed off, dodging around the campers who were riding or leading their horses out of the stable.

Danny, who had just ridden up on Misty, stared after the little girl. "Where's your little sister off to now, Emily? And what's she all excited about this time?"

"Don't ask," Caro said before Emily could reply. "You really don't want to know!"

Emily led Joker out of his stall and swung up into the saddle. "Laura's all excited because she's decided she's going to be part of our act for Parents'

Night," she sighed. "She's on her way to tell her father."

"Yes, and she even has our program all figured out," Caro said. "A musical version of *Peter Rabbit!* And guess who wants to play the starring role?"

"Did I just hear what I think I just heard?" Libby joined them, leading Foxy. "You're kidding, right? Tell me you're kidding!"

Emily shook her head sadly. "Caro's not kidding, Libby. That's exactly what Laura said. And if that's what Laura wants, you can bet that Mr. Frick is going to see that she gets it."

Caro stamped off in the direction of the stable entrance, Vic ambling at her heels. "Well, if we're going to have to put on a third-grade play and hop around singing silly songs in bunny ears, count me out! I'd *die* before I'd make a fool of myself in front of Er—uh, my parents and everybody."

"Remember, Laura's just a lonely little girl . . ." Danny began, but Libby cut her off.

"How can she possibly be lonely? She's hanging around us every single minute! When Emily and I agreed to give her riding lessons, we didn't know that we'd all be turned into full-time baby-sitters. That definitely wasn't part of the deal," Libby said, scowling.

"No, it wasn't," Emily agreed. "I think we should talk to Pam. Maybe she can explain how we feel to Matt, and then he can talk to Mr. Frick, and Mr. Frick can talk to Laura."

Danny nodded. "Good idea. Let's talk to Pam at lunch, okay?"

"With Laura sitting right there? I don't think so," Emily said. "She's having lunch with us, remember."

"And probably even supper," Libby sighed. "I wouldn't be surprised if she persuaded Mr. Frick to let her sleep over in the Fillies' bunkhouse one of these nights, too!"

"Hey, girls, get a move on!" Chris Webster, Pam and Warren's younger brother, came into the stable. "Everybody's waiting for you, and Warren wants to get started taping the classes . . . ." He looked at their glum faces. "Something wrong?"

"Wrong?" Libby echoed. "What could possibly be wrong? Everything's perfectly fine." She nudged Foxy with her heels and began heading for the stable door. Emily and Danny followed.

As Emily passed him, Chris said, "You know Mr. Frick's little daughter—that kid named Laura?"

"Yes, I sure do!" Emily said.

"Well, she's going to be one of your bunkmates tonight. I was hanging out with Dad and Mr. Frick a few minutes ago, and she asked them if she could sleep over and they said she could." He grinned. "Better tell Caro—Laura will be sleeping in the empty bunk over hers, and I know Caro doesn't like surprises."

Libby looked back at him over her shoulder. "I don't know about Caro, but somehow *I'm* not surprised!"

"Thanks for warning us, Chris—I mean, telling us," Emily said. As she rode Joker out into the sunshine, she felt as though her "little shadow" was

44

right beside her. *It's not that I don't like Laura,* she thought as she approached the Intermediate riding ring. *I do like her. But I'd like her a lot more if she wasn't always there!*

Emily's riding class was almost over before she realized that for the first time in days, Laura *wasn't* there. After she and Joker finished a perfect round over the jumps, Emily trotted up next to Penny. "Where's Laura?" she asked. "She's usually hanging over the fence or sitting in the bleachers, but now she's not."

"I think she got bored," Penny said. "She went over to the Advanced ring to watch Lynda, Libby, and Caro, and then she disappeared. I don't know where she is."

Emily stood up in her stirrups, craning her neck to look at the Beginners' ring. To her surprise, she saw Laura leaning over the fence watching the younger riders and Dru playing musical chairs—or, in this case, musical hay bales, the way they'd done on Field Day. There wasn't any music. Instead, Rachel, the beginners' instructor, clapped her hands when it was time for the contestants to jump off their mounts and sit down on a bale of hay. Dru was still in the game, along with two Foals. One of them was Jennifer. The Foals who had been eliminated were cheering from the sidelines, and Laura was cheering right along with them while Warren taped the whole scene.

"What's going on over there?" Penny asked as

Emily sat back down on her saddle. "It sounds like a football game or something."

"Nope," Emily said. "Just musical chairs. And guess who's leading the cheering section?" She grinned. "Laura, that's who."

Penny brightened. "Gee, Emily, do you think maybe she's getting tired of doing everything with the Fillies?"

"I wouldn't be surprised. Wouldn't it be neat if she decided to join the Beginners' class? That would let Libby and me off the hook!"

But when riding class was over, Laura was waiting by the gate of the Intermediate ring, seated on Donna's back while Dru held the mare's reins.

"Look at me!" Laura cried as Emily, Penny, and Danny came out with the other riders. "Dru said I could ride Donna back to the stable! Isn't that neat? Dru won musical chairs, and Jennifer came in second. And I'm going to help Dru rub Donna down and cool him off, aren't I, Dru?"

Dru nodded and began leading Donna away. Emily and Joker kept pace with them as Emily said enthusiastically, "I was watching part of the Beginners' class, Laura. It sure looked like fun! You know something? I bet you'd be good at musical chairs, maybe even better than Jennifer. Wouldn't you like to show the Foals how well you can ride?"

"Oh, no," Laura said. "I'd much rather have private lessons with you and Libby! And Emily, guess what? I asked Daddy and Mr. Webster if I could sleep over in the Fillies' cabin tonight, and they said okay! That means I can go to campfire and everything. I can't wait to go to campfire! Won't it be fun?"

"Yeah—fun," Emily said sadly.

"And after my lessons, I'll start teaching you the *Peter Rabbit* songs. They're not hard at all. Hey, Dru, can you make Donna go a little faster? I won't fall off if she trots."

"The *Peter Rabbit* songs?" Dru looked up at her, puzzled.

"I'll tell you all about it when we get back to the stable," Laura said. "Now, will you please make Donna trot?"

"Yes, Dru, why don't you do that?" Emily suggested. She saw Libby, Caro, and Lynda coming toward them on their horses. All three were wearing long faces, and Emily thought that even the horses looked unhappy. "We'll be there in a minute."

"Whee!" Laura sang out as Dru obediently started jogging and Donna picked up her pace.

The six remaining Fillies waited until they were sure Laura couldn't hear them. Then Caro said, "Libby told us that Laura's spending the night in our cabin—and in the bunk over mine! We won't be able to close our eyes—I bet that kid even talks in her sleep!"

"I think it's time we rebelled," Lynda said. "I know she's the apple of Mr. Frick's eye, and we want to keep him happy because he's Matt's new partner and he's doing a lot of good things for Webster's, but enough is enough! Somebody just has to tell Laura that she can't always have everything she wants."

"That's not going to be easy," Penny said.

Libby made a face. "Tell me about it! Any time anybody suggests something she doesn't want to do, she just says, 'Oh, no,' and does exactly what she likes. Like my grandmother says, 'You can lead a horse to water but you can't make him drink.' "

Suddenly Emily had an idea. "What if you had a really *stubborn* horse, one that was really contrary? And you knew he was thirsty, but he wouldn't drink because it was your idea, not his?"

Danny looked at her, frowning. "But we're not talking about horses. We're talking about Laura."

"I know that." Emily was grinning now. "What I'm trying to say is that we keep trying to talk Laura into getting to know the Foals and make friends with some of the girls her own age, right? But she keeps saying all she wants to do is hang out with the Fillies. What if we started telling her just the opposite? That we *don't* want her to do anything with anybody but us?"

"Emily, I think you've got something there!" Libby said, her eyes sparkling with mischief. "We tell her that because she's the Fillies' mascot, she has to stick to us like glue!"

"You mean we make her do *everything* with us? Chores, too?" Penny asked.

"*Especially* chores," Caro said. "And not just stable chores, either. She likes those. I think we have to show Laura that being a Filly isn't all play and no work." She was grinning, too.

But Danny shook her head. "I don't know. When we tried to put one over on Mr. Frick, it backfired.

That's how we got stuck with Laura in the first place."

"Yes, but this time, we'll be doing exactly what Mr. Frick wants," Emily pointed out. "And what Laura wants—or thinks she wants, anyway."

"There's just one thing," Caro said. "How are we going to get around *Peter Rabbit?* I meant what I said—no way am I going to act like a bunny on Parents' Night!"

"We'll think of something," Emily assured her. "And now we'd better get going, or Laura will send out a search party for us."

As they started riding toward the stable, she added, "Remember, from now on, Laura has *seven* big sisters, and we're not going to let her out of our sight!"

Chapter Five

By the time Emily and the other Fillies had started unsaddling and rubbing down their mounts, everyone else except Laura and Dru had finished and was heading for the farmhouse.

"Where have you been?" Laura whined. "Dru and I thought maybe you got lost or something. And I'm awful hungry!"

Lynda gave her a great big smile. "We had something to talk about. And guess what it was?"

"What?" Laura asked, immediately interested.

"*You,* that's what," Emily told her.

"Really?" The little girl's face lit up. "What about me?"

"Oh, lots of things." Emily stuck her head out of Joker's stall and called down to Penny, "Penny, I think you ought to tell Dru what we decided."

As Penny took Dru aside, Laura said, "Isn't anyone going to tell *me?*"

"We sure are," Caro said, "just as soon as we take care of our horses."

Laura danced from stall to stall, so curious she could hardly stand it. When at last all their mounts had been attended to and the girls were on their way out of the stable, Libby fell into step beside Laura and put an arm around her shoulders.

"Like Emily told you, you're the Fillies' mascot, right?"

Laura nodded eagerly. "Right! Only I don't know what a mascot is supposed to do."

"That's one of the things we were talking about," Libby said. "Because the Fillies have never had a mascot before, we realized that we didn't really know, either. But now we do."

"Yes, Laura." Emily came up on the other side of Laura. "We figured out exactly what your duties are going to be."

Laura frowned. "Duties?"

"You know—your responsibilities," Danny put in. "All the campers at Webster's have things they have to do, whether they like them or not. And there are rules everybody has to follow."

"Oh, I know about those! Like taking care of your horse, and helping Marie with meals, and—"

"And lots of other things," Emily said. "Things you wouldn't know about because you haven't been here all season. Things like making your bunk neatly every morning, and cleaning the cabin every day, and taking your turn in the garden, and being on dish detail."

Laura nodded happily. "That all sounds like fun! Can I do all those things, too?"

"Absolutely!" Caro said sweetly and smiled. "As

a matter of fact, we decided that because you're our mascot, we're going to let you help us with all our chores. From now on, you're going to help us with *everything*. But there's only one catch."

"What is it?"

"You have to spend *all* your time with us. And whatever we tell you to do, you have to do it. That's what mascots are for."

Laura beamed. "Oh, goody! That's exactly what I want to do!"

"Then, let's start right now," Emily said. "Since you're going to be sleeping over in our bunkhouse tonight, the bunk over Caro's has to be made up. There aren't any sheets or blankets or anything on it, because nobody has slept there since my friend Judy visited us a while back. You'll have to ask Marie to give you all the stuff you need."

"Okay, I'll ask her right after lunch."

"Oh, no," Lynda said. "You'd better ask her right away, because I happen to know she's going into town as soon as lunch is served, and she won't be back until it's time to start preparing supper."

Laura frowned. "But I'm *hungry.*"

"I'm sure there'll be something left when you finish making up your bunk," Libby said. "All the bunks are supposed to be made up before lunch. It's a rule."

"Oh." Laura sighed. "Okay. I'll do it right now."

"We'll save you a sandwich," Emily assured her. "Or at least *part* of a sandwich. You can't be *too* hungry since you had two breakfasts this morning."

"We Fillies have to watch our weight," Dru

added, eyeing Laura's plump little figure. "I was really fat when I first came to camp, but Caro put me on a diet right away."

Caro nodded smugly. "I sure did. And just look at her now! You know, I bet if you're very careful about what you eat, you could lose a pound or two over the next few days." She turned to Emily. "Forget about the sandwich. We'll make Laura a nice, nourishing salad—lots of lettuce and tomatoes and carrots topped off with a handful of alfalfa sprouts. Ham and cheese on rye is *much* too fattening."

"But I *love* ham and cheese on rye," Laura said. "And cookies, and brownies, and ice-cream sundaes. I don't like salads at all. My mother *never* makes me eat salad."

Libby shook her head sadly. "Well, suit yourself. But if you're serious about being the Fillies' mascot, remember what Caro said—you have to do whatever we say. Believe me, we know what's best for you. Of course, if you *don't* want to be our mascot, just say so. We'll understand."

"Oh, no! I'll do what you tell me to because you and Emily are my big sisters." Laura's smile returned. "I'm going to find Marie now. But when you make my salad, go easy on the alfalfa sprouts, okay? I tried them once, and it was just like eating *hair*!"

Emily patted her on the back. "Good for you. And remember, Laura, *all* the Fillies are your big sisters now, and big sisters always know best."

Lunch was almost over when Laura came trotting into the dining room. She slid into the empty chair

53

at the Fillies' table and looked at the plate Dru set in front of her. It was piled high with fresh vegetables and greens and delicately sprinkled with alfalfa sprouts. After a moment's hesitation, Laura picked up her fork and dug in. While chomping a mouthful of salad, she said, "I'm awful thirsty. May I please have some milk?"

Pam, who had been let in on the girls' plan, said, "Sure. Here you go." She handed Laura a tall glass, and Laura took a big gulp.

"Yuck!" She made a face and put down the glass. "What *is* this? It doesn't taste like milk."

"It's *skim* milk," Dru told her. "Less than one percent butter fat. Much healthier and not nearly as fattening as whole milk. I drink it all the time."

Laura looked at her skeptically. "Do you like it?"

"Not much," Dru admitted. "But I drink it anyway."

"And we saved you something special for dessert," Penny told her.

Laura's eyes lit up. "Oh, boy! What is it?"

"A big, fat, red apple!" Danny set it down in front of her. "Isn't it beautiful? It was picked this morning from one of the trees in the orchard."

"Gee, that's . . . nice." But Laura didn't sound very enthusiastic.

Suddenly a lot of whispers and squeals were heard coming from the Foals' table as the door to the kitchen opened. Melinda came into the dining room carrying a luscious-looking chocolate frosted cake on a platter. Ten candles flickered merrily as she crossed the room, and everybody applauded.

She set it down in front of one of the Foals while the others began singing at the top of their lungs:

"Happy birthday to you!
Happy birthday to you!
Happy birthday, dear Betsy,
Happy birthday to you!"

Laura's eyes grew big as saucers. "Oh, wow!" she exclaimed. "I just *love* chocolate cake!"

"Only the icing is chocolate," Lynda informed her. "The cake is just plain yellow, with raspberry jam between the layers."

"Raspberry jam . . ." Laura sighed. "I *love* raspberry jam!"

Betsy blew out all her candles and began slicing the cake. Laura watched her every move. "You don't suppose there'll be any left over, do you?" she asked wistfully.

"Probably not. And even if there were, the Foals would get it for dessert tonight," Emily said.

"Yes—Foals don't have to worry about their weight the way we older girls do," Dru added. "Foals eat *anything*. Aren't you glad you're not a Foal?"

"Oh, yes," Laura said, shoving another forkful of lettuce and sprouts into her mouth. But she didn't look very glad, Emily noticed with satisfaction.

"Have a slice of this delicious whole-grain bread," Libby suggested. She passed the bread to Laura, who took a piece and reached for the butter.

"No butter," Caro said sternly. "*Very* high in saturated fats. Not good for you at all."

"But I *like* butter," Laura said. "*Lots* of butter." She looked around at the Fillies' disapproving faces. "Oh, okay. No butter." She took a big bite out of her piece of bread and munched in silence.

"That's the best cake I ever had!" Jennifer sang out from the Foals' table. "Can I have another piece?"

As Melinda handed her a slice, Laura almost choked on her butterless whole-grain bread.

Back in the bunkhouse after lunch, all the Fillies busied themselves with various activities. The sky had clouded over, so nobody went outside to sunbathe. Danny curled up in her bunk with a book, Lynda put on her earphones and listened to a tape of rock music, Libby announced that she was going to take a nap, and Caro began polishing her toenails. Emily took out her stationery and started a letter to Judy, while Penny and Dru took out Dru's Monopoly set for one of their endless games.

Laura wandered from bunk to bunk, obviously at loose ends.

"What're you reading, Danny?" she asked.

"*The Black Stallion Returns,*" Danny mumbled, absorbed in the story. "Terrific book."

"Oh . . . . What're you listening to, Lynda?"

Lynda blinked. "What? I can't hear very well with these earphones on."

"Oh. Never mind . . . . Hey, Libby, are you really sleeping?"

"Mmmmrf," said Libby, burying her face in her pillow.

"Hey, Caro, that's a really neat color. Can I paint my toenails, too?"

"Maybe, after I'm done."

"Emily, can I have some of your stationery so I can write another letter to Sandy?"

Emily tore off a sheet and handed it to her. "Sure. But you'll have to find a pen."

"Oh . . . . Dru, will you and Penny teach me how to play Monopoly? I don't really like board games much, but it's better than nothing."

"Okay," Dru said, concentrating on her throw of the dice. "You'll have to wait till we've finished this game, though. It'll take about an hour . . . ."

Laura sighed. "I wonder what the other campers are doing?"

"Rachel took the Thoros into town to do some shopping," Caro told her. "And I think the Foals are doing arts and crafts in the Activity Room. They're making a collage for Parents' Weekend."

Laura sighed again. "That sounds like fun." Nobody had anything to say. "Well, maybe I'll take a nap, like Libby." She climbed into the bunk over Caro's.

"Don't jiggle!" Caro ordered.

"Sorry." Laura heaved an even bigger sigh.

Then it began to rain—just a drizzle at first, but it soon turned into a steady downpour.

"The roof leaks," Laura told anyone who happened to be listening. "I'm getting wet."

Nobody seemed to care.

                          *   *   *

The shower proved to be brief, and water sports
were held as usual under watery sunshine in the
Winnepac River. Emily, feeling guilty for having ig-
nored Laura during rest period, kept an eye on the
little girl while she dog paddled in the shallows near
the bank. Libby had volunteered to give Laura the
first of her riding lessons, but Emily came along to
help her saddle Cupcake. Warren, complete with
camcorder, was waiting in the stable yard, ready to
tape the lesson.

Laura trotted the pony around the yard, waving
and grinning at the camera. "Hi, Mommy and
Daddy! Look at me! See what a good rider I am?"

Laura's high spirits had returned with the sunlight and she was her usual cheerful, bouncy self.
Emily watched her ride for a few minutes, then hurried off to join the rest of the Fillies in the Activity
Room. While Laura was otherwise occupied, the Fillies planned to start practicing their barbershop
numbers. When it was Emily's turn to play riding
instructor, Libby would rehearse with the rest of the
girls. Later today, they'd settle the *Peter Rabbit* question once and for all.

Emily was just crossing the farmhouse porch
when Mr. Frick came out the front door. "Well,
well!" he said heartily. "If it isn't one of Laura's big
sisters! And how's my little dumpling doing today?"

His greeting took Emily aback, until she realized
that by "little dumpling" he meant Laura, not her.
"Oh, she's just fine, Mr. Frick," Emily replied.

"Libby's giving Laura her riding lesson right now, and then I'll take over."

Mr. Frick nodded, beaming. "That's great. You know, Laura's having the time of her life this week. Never seen her happier—her mother and I know now that it was a big mistake on our part not to enroll her as a camper this season. But you can bet your life she'll be a Foal next year!"

Emily smiled. "She's already looking forward to it. And I'm glad she's having fun."

"There's just one thing . . . ." Mr. Frick hesitated, and Emily thought, *Uh-oh. What does he want us to do for Laura now?* "Don't think Mrs. Frick and I aren't delighted with the way you and the other Fillies have taken Laura under your wing—we're pleased as punch, no question about that," he went on. "But we were kind of hoping that while she was here, Laura would spend some time with girls her own age, make some new little friends."

Emily's eyes widened. "Oh, Mr. Frick," she began eagerly, but he cut her off.

"I know, I know. Laura's told me that she's the Fillies' mascot, and she's very proud of that. But what I'm trying to say is, I'd appreciate it if you and the other girls would let her join in some of the Foals' activities every now and then."

"*Let* her?" Emily squawked. "Believe me, Mr. Frick . . ."

"I understand how fond you've all become of her—she's an irresistible little rascal—but don't monopolize *all* her time, all right?" He smiled at her.

"Now I'd better be on my way—I want to see how Warren's getting along taping Laura's lesson."

Emily stared after him, shaking her head. "Oh, Mr. Frick," she whispered, "if you only knew!"

Chapter Six

The minute she walked in the door of the Activity Room, Lynda shoved a piece of paper into Emily's hand. "What kept you?" she said, but before Emily could reply, she added, "Never mind. Those are the words to our opening number—we've already gone over it once. We're going to sing it to the tune of 'Down by the Old Mill Stream.' All barbershop groups sing that, and the harmony's easy."

"We decided we're going to be a barbershop quartet *and* a barbershop trio," Danny said. "The quartet will be Lynda, you, Libby, and me, and the trio will be Caro, Penny, and Dru. The quartet sings the first verse and the trio sings the next one, and so on. Get it?"

Emily scanned the lyrics and grinned. "I'll give it a try. These words are much better than the ones we came up with the other night!"

"We think so," Caro said smugly. "Everybody ready? Hit it, Penny!"

Penny, who was standing by the old upright piano in the corner of the room, struck a key with one finger, then dashed over to join Caro and Dru as the quartet (minus Libby) began to sing:

"Down by the Winn-e-pac
Where the ducks quack, quack,
And the wild geese fly
High up in the sky.
It was then I knew
That my dream came true—
I found my horse
At Webster's of course,
Down by the Winn-e-pac!"

"That was just *beautiful*," Dru sighed.
"Now it's our turn," Caro told her. "Don't talk—*sing*."

"Of all the camps there are
It's the best by far,
And the food's just great—
We all clean our plate!
All the girls are swell
And they ride real well.
It's the place for you
If you love horses, too,
Down by the Winn-e-pac!"

"Those last few lines don't quite fit the rhythm," Danny conceded, "but we have a few days to work on it."

63

"*I* think they're perfectly fine," Caro said.

"That's because *you* wrote them," Lynda pointed out, not unkindly. "Okay, let's do it again. Emily, were you singing melody or harmony or what?"

"Or what!" Emily giggled. "Actually, I was trying to sing harmony. I'll try harder."

Time flew by as the Fillies went over the number several more times. Emily was astonished when she glanced at her watch and saw that an hour had passed. "Whoops! Gotta go," she exclaimed. "My turn with Laura. See you later, gang!"

Running toward the stable, she passed Libby on her way to the farmhouse.

"I started teaching her to post," Libby shouted as she raced up the path. "How'd the rehearsal go?"

"Super," Emily shouted back. "We're gonna be a big hit."

"Down with *Peter Rabbit*!" Libby yelled, raising her fist in a power salute.

"Can I sing you my *Peter Rabbit* song now?" Laura asked a little more than an hour later. She and Emily had just come into the Activity Room after Laura's second lesson of the afternoon, to find the Fillies getting ready to leave—the Thoros were scheduled to rehearse their act for Parents' Night until it was time for supper.

"Laura, I think we have to talk about that," Libby said, catching Emily's eye.

"Yes, we definitely do," Emily agreed. "But we can't do it here. Let's all take a walk down to the sheep pasture, okay?"

"Sure. I love looking at those cute little baby lambs!"

Laura skipped along between Emily and Libby, keeping up an endless stream of chatter about her class play and how good she would have been if she had played the lead. When the girls had visited the ewes and lambs and then settled down under the branches of a tall old oak tree, Emily said, "About that play—"

"Won't it be fun?" Laura interrupted. "I'll be Peter, and Lynda can be Mr. McGregor, and Caro can be the mother rabbit, and the rest of you can be Peter's brothers and sisters!"

Emily looked at her solemnly. "Laura, there's something you have to understand. You're the Fillies' mascot, and the Fillies are *old.*"

"*Real* old," Caro said. "Lynda and I are fourteen. That's six years older than you."

"And Emily, Danny, and I are thirteen," Libby added.

"Dru and I are twelve," Penny put in, "going on thirteen."

"So?" Laura said.

"So we're *way* too old for *Peter Rabbit,*" Emily said firmly. "*Peter Rabbit* is for kids—*little* kids, like Foals. If you were a Foal, it would be okay to sing rabbit songs. But you're not. You're the Fillies' mascot, so you have to do whatever the Fillies do. And the Fillies are *not* going to do *Peter Rabbit.*"

"But I *want* to play Peter Rabbit," Laura wailed. "I know all the songs . . . ."

"Too bad you don't like the Foals," Lynda said

65

with a sigh. "I bet they'd just love to have you in their talent show. You'd probably be their biggest star."

"Yeah. I can see it all now—'Webster's Foals present Laura Frick!' " Danny shook her head sadly. "But of course you don't want to desert your big sisters just for a few minutes of glory in the spotlight, with the cheers and applause of the crowd ringing in your ears."

Emily thought she was laying it on a little thick, but Laura's eyes were shining as she pictured the scene.

"And even if you *did* decide to desert us, we really couldn't let you," Libby put in. "I mean, how would it look to have our mascot hanging out with all those little kids? No, Laura, you're an honorary Filly and you'll just have to make the best of it. Like my grandmother says, you made your bed—now lie in it."

The light in Laura's eyes went out. "I *did* make my bed," she said. "And it wasn't easy doing it all by myself, either. And I ate that hairy salad, too. When am I going to have some *fun*?"

"You had your fun for today," Emily said cheerfully. "Two riding lessons, remember?"

"And you went swimming with us, too," Caro reminded her. "Wasn't that fun?"

Laura sighed. "I guess. Only I got water up my nose . . . ."

"That happens to me all the time," Penny said. "You get used to it after a while."

"Hey, guys," Lynda said, "we'd better get

moving—we're on garden detail today, and if we don't pick those veggies pretty soon, supper's going to be late. Let's go."

All the girls got to their feet and headed for the vegetable garden, but Laura lagged behind.

"Come on, Laura," Libby called over her shoulder. "There's work to be done!"

When they reached the garden, Lynda assigned Laura to help Emily, Libby, and Dru pick corn while she, Caro, and Penny tackled the squash, lettuce, and tomatoes, and Danny began picking plump green beans. Because of the rain earlier in the day, the rich soil had turned into thick, gooey mud, which made their job very messy.

"My nice new boots are getting all icky," Laura complained.

"That's no big deal," Libby said. "You can clean them off and polish them when we get back to the cabin. Mine are pretty icky, too."

"So are mine," Emily added. "We'll be tracking mud all over the place. I guess that means we'll have to wash the bunkhouse floor. You can help us, Laura."

Laura stuck out her lower lip. "At home, my mom polishes my shoes and washes the floor."

"Well, you're not at home now," Lynda said. "Don't worry—we'll show you how to do it."

Laura pulled off a few ears of corn and dropped them into a bushel basket, scowling. "Do the Foals have as many chores to do as the Fillies?" she asked.

"Oh, no," Dru replied. "That's because we're

older and more responsible. The Foals don't work *nearly* as hard as we do."

"Oh," Laura said. Then suddenly she screamed.

Alarmed, Emily said, "What is it? What's the matter?"

"A *worm!* There's a big, fat, horrible *worm* climbing up my arm!" the little girl shrieked, jumping up and down in the mud.

"If you'll stand still, I'll pick him off," Lynda said calmly. Laura obeyed, squeezing her eyes shut tightly. "Why, he's not big and horrible at all." Lynda examined the creature with interest as it clung to the tip of her finger. "He's not even a worm. He's a caterpillar, and he's a lovely shade of green with pretty little spots. I bet you scared him half to death."

"He scared *me* half to death," Laura said with a shudder. "I *hate* worms, and I hate caterpillars even more. They have all those nasty little *feet!* Can I open my eyes now? Is he gone?"

"All gone. How about picking some more corn now?"

"Oh, no! I don't want to *touch* that corn," Laura said. "That's where that worm thing came from, and I bet his brothers and sisters live there, too!"

"Honestly, Laura, such a big fuss about one measly little caterpillar!" Caro said from the squash patch.

Danny giggled. "Look who's talking! You had a fit the first time you came across one, remember?"

Caro sniffed. "That was before I learned to appreciate the beauties of nature."

"Then I guess you don't mind that one of those beauties is crawling up your back," Libby said mildly.

"*Yuck!* Get it off me! Help, somebody!" Caro squealed, jumping around exactly as Laura had a moment before.

Everybody broke up, and Libby laughed loudest of all. "Just kidding, Caro. Can't you take a joke?"

"*Some* people have a very peculiar idea of what's funny," Caro snapped. She tossed one last squash into her basket. "There, that ought to do it. I wonder how Marie's planning on cooking the squash tonight?"

"Maybe fritters," Dru suggested. "We haven't had squash fritters all week."

"I never knew there were so many ways to fix squash," Penny said. "Sometimes you can't even tell what it is."

"I'll know what it is," Laura mumbled. "I *hate* squash, and my parents never make me eat anything I don't like. And I'm not going to eat any of that corn, either. A worm might get cooked in it!"

"You don't have to eat the squash or the corn if you don't want to," Emily assured her. "You can have a nice, big salad instead."

"Phooey on salad!" Laura scowled at the baskets full of greens and tomatoes that Caro and Penny were carrying. "And phooey on squash and corn, too! I'm real tired. Can we stop now?"

Lynda nodded. "I think we have enough of everything. Laura, you can take my basket and I'll help carry the corn—it's too heavy for you. If we hurry,

69

we'll just have time to wash off the mud before supper. We can wash the floor afterward."

Laura plodded off with a big basket of lettuce, not waiting to see if the other girls were coming. Emily gazed after her, feeling sorry for the little girl. She also felt kind of guilty, but she told herself, *We're not really being mean to her. We're not asking her to do anything we're not doing. And sooner or later she's going to figure out that she doesn't have to stick with us every single minute, and she'll have a lot more fun with the Foals.* But she ran after Laura, anyway, lugging her basket of corn.

"Hey, Laura, wait up!" she called. Laura stopped and Emily caught up with her. "Don't forget about campfire tonight. There'll be a singalong, and maybe some games, too. You'll enjoy that."

"Will we toast marshmallows?" Laura asked, looking more cheerful. "And if we do, can I eat some?"

"Sure you can. We might even make s'mores."

Now Laura beamed. "Oh, boy! I *love* s'mores! That sounds like fun—I can hardly wait!"

But after supper—and after washing the cabin floor, showering, and changing their clothes—when the Fillies were ready to go to the campfire, Laura wasn't. She had climbed up into her bunk "just for a little rest," and had fallen sound asleep. Emily and Libby tried to wake her up, but Laura just buried her head under the pillow.

Libby looked at Emily and shrugged. "Well, we tried."

Emily nodded, and, one by one, the girls tiptoed out of the bunkhouse, leaving their mascot to her dreams.

Chapter Seven

Emily was awakened the following morning by somebody shaking her shoulders and shouting in her ear. She tried to ignore it, but whoever it was wouldn't go away. Finally, she opened her eyes, to see Libby bending over her, with her short, curly red hair standing on end and a frantic expression on her freckled face.

"Emily!" Libby cried. "You've got to get up! She's gone!"

Emily blinked sleepily. "Gone? Who's gone?" Then she groaned. "Don't tell me Dru ran away again!" She hadn't given much thought to Dru and her worries about her parents because there had been so many other things to think about, but it was entirely possible that Dru had been more upset than she'd let on.

"No, not me. I'm right here," Dru said, plopping down on Emily's bunk.

"Then who . . . ?"

"Laura, that's who! The Fillies' mascot has flown

the coop!" Libby said. "And we've got to find her, or Mr. Frick will *kill* us!"

Emily sat bolt upright. "Omigosh! You're kidding! Tell me you're kidding!"

"We're not kidding," Pam sighed. "I was the first one up this morning, and I happened to glance over at Laura's bunk. It was empty. She's gone, all right."

"Oh, wow!" Emily leaped out of bed and began getting dressed. "Libby's right—if anything happens to Laura, Mr. Frick *will* kill us. Where could she have gone?"

"I haven't the slightest idea," Pam said, "but we have to find her and bring her back. I want each of you girls to look in a different area around the camp. She can't have gone very far. I'll search, too. If we don't find her before breakfast, we are in *very* big trouble!"

"I did it again," Emily moaned. "Me and my bright ideas! All I wanted to do was make Laura realize that she'd have a better time with the Foals than with the Fillies, but I guess she got so miserable that she couldn't stand it anymore. It's all my fault!"

"No, it's not," Lynda said. "We were all responsible for Laura."

"And we're all responsible for finding her," Libby added. "I'll check out the sheep pasture." She ran out the door, Danny at her heels.

"I'll look in the picnic grove," Danny called back.

"Come on, Lynda," Caro said, throwing on a hooded sweatshirt. "I'll take the dock and the boathouse, and you go to the mares' and foals' pasture!"

"Penny and I will look in the stables," Dru said.

"That's where I hid when I ran away that time. Maybe we'll trip over Laura the way Emily tripped over me!" They dashed out of the cabin.

Pam clutched her head. "I can't *believe* this!" she said. "It was bad enough losing Dru a few weeks ago. Now we've lost another one, and it's Dad's partner's daughter this time! This has been one heck of a summer!"

Emily, fully dressed now, went over to Pam and touched her arm. "Pam, I'm really sorry. It *is* all my fault. I feel just awful about it!" She tried to swallow the huge lump in her throat. "Fine big sister I turned out to be! I wouldn't blame you and Matt and Marie if you didn't let me come back to Webster's next year. I'm a *menace*!"

Pam managed to smile, and gave her a quick hug. "Don't be silly, Emily. You're not a menace. I'm supposed to be in charge of the Fillies, and if anyone messed up, it's me. Now pull yourself together and get moving. I'm going to look, too. We'll find her. I know we will!"

But, half an hour later, nobody had found Laura. Pam and the Fillies gathered in front of their bunkhouse, and every face was the picture of gloom. The breakfast bell had already rung, summoning the campers to the dining room.

"Well, girls," Pam said grimly, "I guess it's time to face the music. I'll tell Mom and Dad, and they'll have to decide where we go from here."

"She was such a *nice* little girl," Danny murmured,

73

wiping away a tear. "So cute and bubbly and every-thing. And she was only eight years old!"

"Danny!" Libby shouted. "Stop talking about her as if she were *dead!* And don't tell us about some book you read about a kid who met some terrible fate!"

"Well, there *was* this story—" Danny began, but Caro cut her off.

"Danny, we don't want to hear about it, okay? Don't you ever read anything cheerful?"

"Sometimes," Danny mumbled. But she didn't say anything else.

Silently the Fillies followed Pam to the farm-house. She hesitated for a moment outside the door to the dining room, then squared her shoulders and marched in, seven sorrowful-looking girls strag-gling behind her.

And then she stopped so suddenly that Emily, who was next in line, ran right into her. "What . . ." Emily began.

"Hi, Pam! Hi, Emily! Guess what? I'm having breakfast with the Foals today!" Laura was seated next to Jennifer at the Foals' table. In front of her was a huge stack of waffles drenched in maple syrup. "You're all such sleepyheads that I couldn't wait for you to wake up," Laura went on. "I was *starving,* so I came right here, and Mrs. Webster let me help make the waffles and everything! And the Foals were on breakfast detail, so we all cooked breakfast together. Isn't that neat?"

"Neat," Pam whispered. "Real neat." She and the Fillies clustered around the Foals' table, gazing down at Laura as though they'd never seen her before.

Laura looked from face to face as she shoveled a forkful of waffles into her mouth. "What's wrong?" she asked. "You're not mad at me or anything, are you? I mean, Emily usually gets up real early to go see Joker and I was going to tell her where I was going, only today she didn't, so I didn't. And I missed campfire and everything, and I didn't eat much for supper, so my stomach was rumbling like anything! So I got dressed and I came here and I met Jennifer and she introduced me to the other Foals and guess what? They want me to do my *Peter Rabbit* song in their talent show for Parents' Night! So I'm sorry, but I guess I can't be the Fillies' mascot anymore. Is that okay?"

Pam reached out and patted Laura's head. "Yes, Laura, it's okay."

Emily took a deep breath. "I think what I need now is a waffle. Maybe two. And a *gallon* of maple syrup!"

From then on, Laura spent all her time at Webster's with her new friends. Though Emily and Libby offered to continue giving her daily riding lessons, Laura announced that she'd decided to join the Beginners' class with Jennifer, the other Foals, and Dru. And when Dru told the Fillies that Laura won musical chairs the very first time she played, nobody was a bit surprised.

Now that the problem of Laura was safely and happily settled, Emily and her friends were free to concentrate on polishing their horsemanship skills and on rehearsing their act for Parents' Night. Besides "Down by the Winnepac," they had worked up another number, a version of "Sweet Adeline" called "Sweet Horse of Mine." Now, during rest period, Emily and Libby put their heads together and came up with a third song, a variation on "A Bicycle Built for Two."

Before they sang it for the rest of the Fillies, however, Emily told them, "There's just one hitch—we really ought to be singing this song to a horse, or it won't be funny."

Caro laughed. "Oh, I know what you're up to! You just want to get Joker into the act!"

"Emily, you're out of your tree," Lynda said. "The show's going to be in the Activity Room. Matt and Marie would never allow us to bring a horse into the house."

"Maybe and maybe not," Libby said with an impish grin. "Listen to the song, and then we'll tell you our idea. Ready, Emily?"

Emily nodded, and they began:

"Daisy, Daisy, give us a ride, please do!
We're horse crazy all for the love of you.
Your coat is so sleek and shiny,
Your dainty hooves are tiny,
And we'll look sweet
Upon the seat
Of a standardbred built for two!"

"There are two other verses, but we won't sing them for you now," Emily said. "You get the picture, though. Without a horse, it'll fall flat."

"So, since we can't use a *real* horse," Libby said, "we thought we'd *make* one. You know—a horse costume with a couple of people in it? Or maybe even *three* people?" She looked meaningfully at Caro, Penny, and Dru, the members of the barbershop trio.

"No way!" Caro said at once. "No way in the world am I going to be the rear end of a horse! That'd be worse than being a dopey rabbit!"

"Who said anything about the rear end?" Emily asked. "Since you're the tallest, we were thinking of you for the front, with Penny in the middle and Dru at the end."

Penny giggled. "I think that would be fun! You wouldn't mind, would you, Dru?"

"I don't care," Dru said, sighing. "My folks probably won't come anyway, so it doesn't matter what I do."

"Well, *my* parents are coming and so is Eric," Caro said. "It's bad enough that I'll have to dress up like a guy and wear a handlebar moustache—if I'm part of a horse, Eric will laugh his head off!"

"He probably will," Emily agreed. "But he'll love it. He'll think it's terrific that you're such a good sport."

"You really think so?" Caro sounded doubtful.

"No question about it," Emily said firmly. "Let's see—what can we use for the horse's body?"

"How about the blanket from Laura's bunk?"

Danny suggested. "It's big and brown." She reached up into the bunk over Caro's and pulled the blanket down.

"And we could borrow Marie's mop, the one I used for my witch wig in the Costume Parade at Field Day," Dru said, getting into the spirit of things. "That would make a good tail."

"For the head, we could use a big brown grocery bag," Lynda said. "If we stuffed it with newspapers and kind of shaped it a little, we could draw eyes and nostrils on it and glue on cardboard ears!"

"And the 'horse' could wear one of the ponies' bridles—that ought to be just the right size," Penny added.

"You and Dru and Caro could wear your barbershop costumes underneath so you wouldn't have to change," Libby put in. "And while the quartet is singing, you guys could do a little dance!"

"Oh, sure—a six-legged horse!" Caro scoffed. But Emily thought she seemed to be weakening.

"Why don't we see if anybody's using the Activity Room?" Lynda said. "If it's empty, we could run through the horse number with just the blanket— that's the important part for you horse people to get used to."

"Horse people! *Really!*" Caro said with a groan. She didn't object, though.

The Fillies were on their way out the door when they saw Pam striding toward them. She flung out her arms and said, "Hold it, girls! Where are you off to?"

"The Activity Room," Libby told her. "We want to practice our new number for Parents' Night."

"Sorry—the Thoros are rehearsing in there. Besides, I need you for a while. Or rather, my brother the photographer needs you."

"What for?" Emily asked.

"Well, he was running the tapes he's shot so far for Mom and Dad and Mr. Frick, and they all decided that it doesn't look as though the campers are having enough fun."

"I don't get it—everything we do at Webster's is fun!" Libby said.

"They don't seem to think it looks that way," Pam said. "There's lots of footage of everybody doing kitchen chores, and stable chores, and having riding lessons and swimming lessons and all that stuff, but there aren't any scenes of the girls just goofing off—horsing around, you might say. Mr. Frick says if we want to attract more campers next year, we have to show them that not every minute of a camper's day is programmed, and Mom and Dad agreed. That's where you come in."

Dru frowned, puzzled. "Where?"

Pam grinned. "Dad asked me to round up some campers, *any* campers, so Warren could tape them just hanging out or fooling around. Naturally, I thought of the Fillies."

"Gee, thanks, Pam!" Lynda said wryly. "Because we're better at hanging out and fooling around than the Thoros or the Foals, right?"

"That *did* enter my mind," Pam teased. "Actually, though, since the Foals are on a nature walk with

Melinda and the Thoros are rehearsing their skit, you were the only ones available. Want to do it?"

"I think it's a cool idea!" Libby said. "How about if I juggle pinecones? I've been practicing—I can keep five of them in the air at once. And I've gotten real good at hanging by my knees from the lowest branch of that tree over there. Maybe Warren would like to tape that."

"Yeah, and Danny and I could put on our shorts and be sunbathing while Libby's showing off," Lynda said.

"*Goofing* off," Libby corrected. "I bet I'm the best goofer-offer at Webster's!"

Danny said, "And after that, I could read aloud to Libby and Lynda from *National Velvet*. Just a couple of pages—not a whole chapter," she added quickly.

"Dru and I could go visit the sheep and the baby lambs," Penny put in. "We do that whenever we have a chance."

"Yes, and one of the lambs is my special friend," Dru said. "He's not scared of me at all."

"Emily, let's go down to the stable," Caro suggested. "Remember how you took those pictures of Joker and me when we first came to camp? You could bring your Polaroid and take some more in the stable yard. Got any film?"

"I think so," Emily said.

"That all sounds terrific." Pam beamed at them all. "I'll go find Warren—he can start with Lynda, Libby, and Danny, then follow Penny and Dru to the sheep pasture and wind up with Emily, Caro, and Joker down at the stable."

As she hurried off, Emily said to Caro, "Forget about the camera. I just had a much better idea!"

Caro gave her a look. "I don't know, Emily. Somehow your ideas always seem to get us in trouble."

"This one won't. Come on—I'll tell you about it on the way."

"Cut!" Warren shouted a little while later. "Okay, Emily, I have enough footage of you and Caro braiding honeysuckle into Joker's mane."

"Did you get some good close-ups?" Emily asked eagerly.

Caro ran a hand over her smooth blond hair. "I hope they were all of my good side!"

"Not close-ups of you, silly. Of *Joker*," Emily said.

"Plenty of close-ups. Are you going to do anything else? I'd like some action," Warren told the girls.

"We'll give you action!" Emily turned to Caro. "Remember what we decided?"

"Of course." Caro climbed up on the fence to which Joker was tethered and slid onto his bare back.

Emily climbed up next. "Make room for me," she said, and Caro reluctantly wriggled toward the rear so Emily could sit in front. "Is the mike turned on, Warren?" Emily asked. When he nodded, she glanced over her shoulder at Caro. "Ready?" she whispered.

Caro grinned. "Ready!"

81

Gently nudging the big palomino with her heels, Emily spoke loudly and clearly as he began to amble around the stable yard. "This isn't the way we're taught to ride at Webster's, and you shouldn't do it either because you might fall off—unless you're very good riders, like Caro and me. But right now, we're just horsing around! And now we want to sing a song I made up. . . ."

Caro whispered in her ear, and Emily said, "Just for the record, my friend Libby and I made up the first verse, but Caro helped with the second one."

Mugging at the camcorder, Caro said, "Actually, I made up *most* of the second verse, but Emily helped!"

"Whatever. Anyway, here goes!" And they both began to sing:

"Joker, Joker, give us a ride, please do!
We're horse crazy, all for the love of you.
Your coat is so sleek and shiny,
Your dainty hooves are tiny,
And we look sweet
Upon the seat
Of a standardbred built for two!"

Joker nodded his head up and down and did a little dance step, making Caro squeal and grab Emily around the waist. When they had settled themselves again, they launched into the second verse, the one they'd created while Warren was filming the other Fillies:

"Joker, Joker, treasure of purest gold!
We'll still love you even when you grow old."

Emily sang the next two lines by herself:

"Of all the Webster's horses
Joker the best of course is."

Caro joined her for the rest of the song:

"But you'll look sweet
Upon the seat
Of the horse that's assigned to you!"

Pam, who had been leaning over the fence watching and listening, laughed and clapped, and even Warren smiled as he turned off the camcorder. "You two are something else, you know?" he said.
Caro smirked. "We know!"

Chapter Eight

"Are you *sure* your folks and Eric are going to arrive in time for supper?" Caro fretted on Friday afternoon. She had just changed her clothes for the fourth time, and was peering at her reflection in the mirror over the bureau in the Fillies' bunkhouse, adjusting the neckline of her hand-embroidered peasant blouse. "What do you think, Emily? On the shoulder or off the shoulder?"

Emily cocked her head to one side and looked critically at Caro. "Yes, I'm sure they're going to be here in time for supper—unless they get a flat or something, that is—and, *on* the shoulder," she said. "You have white streaks from your strap marks and they don't show when you keep the blouse pulled up."

Caro frowned. "You're right. Only, if you don't see the strap marks, you don't know how tanned I really am. Maybe I ought to wear something else. . . ."

"I'm glad *my* boyfriend isn't coming," Danny said,

84

looking up from the boot she was polishing. "I wouldn't want to try on all those clothes."

Penny stared at her. "I didn't know you had a boyfriend!"

Danny shrugged. "I don't. But if I did, I'd be glad he wasn't coming."

"My parents are supposed to arrive tomorrow morning in time for my riding class," Penny said. "They're real proud that I'm an Intermediate. They thought I'd be a Beginner because I hadn't ridden that much before I came to Webster's."

"My folks probably won't be able to come until Sunday, for the horse show," Danny said. "They wanted to be here for Parents' Night, but Dad had to go on a business trip."

"Mom and Dad wouldn't miss Parents' Night for anything," Caro said. "They're coming tomorrow afternoon. I can't wait to introduce them to Eric . . ." she smiled at Emily " . . . and you, and Mr. and Mrs. Jordan. I bet our folks will get along real well."

Dru sighed. It was a very loud sigh, one the rest of the Fillies couldn't possibly miss.

"Don't worry, Dru," Lynda said. "They'll turn up, I know they will."

"No, you don't," Dru mumbled, curling up into a little ball on her bunk. *Nobody* knows. I don't know, so how could you?"

Libby, who had been hanging by her knees from her bunk over Emily's, righted herself and leaped down to the floor. "Hey, Dru, I've got a great idea! If your folks don't show, you can come home with

Gram and Grandpa and me! We'll adopt you, okay?"

Dru glowered at her. "Very funny!" She rolled over onto her stomach, burying her face in her folded arms. "If they were coming, somebody would have let me know. They're probably going to my sisters' camp, or my brother's. They've probably even forgotten that I'm at Webster's . . . ."

A brisk knock at the cabin door distracted everyone's attention from Dru's sorrowful droning.

"Who's there?" Emily called out.

"It's me—Chris. That you, Emily?"

Emily went over and peered through the screen. "It's me, all right. What's up?"

"Your folks just got here," he told her. "They're up at the house talking to Mom and Dad."

"Oh, no!" Caro wailed. "They're *early!* My hair's a *mess,* and I just *have* to change this skirt—it makes me look like a *tank!* Don't bring them here till I'm ready, Emily, please?"

Emily shrugged. "You look fine to me, but okay. I'll stall them. Gee, they made great time! It's only a little after five o'clock." She ran over to the mirror and ran her fingers through her short, wavy brown hair. "I was going to put on another shirt, but I guess this one looks all right."

As she dashed out of the cabin and jogged with Chris toward the farmhouse, Emily felt a little funny—both glad and sad. The glad part was because she loved her parents and Eric, and was looking forward to seeing them. The sad part was because they had come to take her home. She hadn't

86

let herself think too much about the end of camp. It meant saying good-bye to all her friends at Webster's—and to Joker. But, on the other hand, it also meant that in just a few days she and Judy would be together again. Then they could start making plans for next summer, when they'd *both* be at Webster's!

"I don't think you'll have to worry about how to keep your family from barging in on Caro," Chris said, interrupting Emily's thoughts. "Looks like they're gonna be tied up for a while."

Looking ahead, Emily saw her mother and father and Eric on the farmhouse porch—and a small, bouncy figure that could only be Laura Frick. As usual, Laura was talking a mile a minute. Her shrill voice carried in the still, late-afternoon air.

"I know who you are," Laura was saying. "I heard Mr. and Mrs. Webster say! You're Emily's mom and dad and Caro's boyfriend! I'm Laura. Emily told you about me, didn't she? About how I was the Fillies' mascot? Well, I'm not anymore, because I have a whole bunch of new friends. I'm kind of a Foal now, only not really, but that's okay because next summer I'll be a *real* Foal and my friend Jennifer and I are going to be here for the whole season! Isn't that neat? Oh, hi, Chris, hi, Emily! I just met your parents and Eric. Caro's right—Eric's *lots* more handsome than Warren."

"I'm outta here," Chris mumbled, scooting around the group and into the house.

Emily pretended not to notice Eric's bright red face as she flung her arms around her mother and father and then gave her brother a quick hug. "You got here so soon," she cried. "That's terrific! Mom, you look great. But your hair's different—shorter. I like it. Dad, you're so *tanned*! And, Eric—you're, well, *taller* or something." She looked at him more closely. "And you're growing a *moustache*!" There were really only a few straggly dark hairs on Eric's upper lip, but obviously he was working on it.

"Honey, it's so good to see you!" Mrs. Jordan said. "Even though we were only here a few weeks ago, you look different, too. Older. Lots older."

"And even prettier than you were the last time we saw you," Mr. Jordan added, smiling.

"Hey, I think you look exactly the same," Eric teased. "You're still my dopey little sister."

"Emily, aren't you going to talk to me?" Laura asked, tugging at Emily's T-shirt. "You're not mad at me or anything, are you?"

Emily grinned down at the little girl. "Why should I be mad at you?"

"Because I'm not the Fillies' mascot anymore. And because you and Libby aren't giving me riding lessons anymore. And because . . ."

"Laura," Emily said solemnly, "I am *not* mad at you. I didn't talk to you right away because I wanted to say hello to my family first." Turning to her parents, she added, "Wait till you see Laura in the Foals' talent show on Parents' Night. She's going to sing a *Peter Rabbit* song that'll knock your socks off!"

"*Peter Rabbit*?" Eric echoed, looking far from enthusiastic.

"You'll love it," Laura said, beaming. "I have ears and a cottontail and everything! And I hop a lot!"

Before anyone could comment on the treat that was in store for them, Jennifer came around the corner of the farmhouse, calling, "Laura! Come on! The Foals are setting up the tables for supper, and you're my partner."

"Coming," Laura shouted. To Emily and her family, she said, "And guess what? Tonight, when the Fillies and the Thoros are going on their moonlight trail ride, me and the Foals are gonna make *popcorn balls!* And I'm sleeping over in the Foals' cabin. Daddy bought me this neat sleeping bag with ducks all over it because there aren't any extra bunks, and I'm going to sleep on the *floor*! It was really nice meeting you, Mr. Jordan and Mrs. Jordan and Eric. See you later, Emily!"

"That kid talks a lot, doesn't she?" Eric said as Laura sprinted off to join Jennifer.

"She's absolutely adorable," Mrs. Jordan said. Then she grinned at Emily. "But I can see how she just might drive you and the Fillies right up the wall."

"Up the wall and over the roof," Emily sighed. She put an arm around her father's waist. "I think it's safe to go to my cabin now." She glanced at Eric. "Caro had to change her outfit for the twenty-seventh time so she'd be absolutely *perfect* when you arrived."

Eric stroked his upper lip. "Do you think she likes men with moustaches?" he asked, his voice almost a whisper. "Maybe this wasn't such a good idea."

"We've never discussed moustaches, but I have a very strong feeling that she's going to be thrilled!"

Caro was. She let out a little shriek the minute Emily and her family came into the bunkhouse. "Oh, Eric!" she cried, her beautifully made-up eyes widening. "You look so *old!*"

Eric turned beet red. "And you look . . . *you* look very nice," he said lamely, but it was clear from his expression that he thought she looked absolutely gorgeous. Caro had rejected both the skirt and peasant blouse in favor of a pale blue flowered dress with puffy sleeves and a flounced hem which Caro had told Emily was a Sarah Finley designer original. Emily didn't know who Sarah Finley was, but Caro had seemed to think she should, so she hadn't said anything. It was a very pretty dress, though, and Caro looked very pretty in it.

Now Caro was blushing, too, as she realized that she hadn't said a word to Emily's mother and father. "Hi, Mr. and Mrs. Jordan," she said, giving them one of her most dazzling smiles. "It's so nice to see you again!"

"Good to see you, too, Caro," Mr. Jordan said, and Mrs. Jordan added, "What a lovely dress! It's a Sarah Finley, isn't it?"

"Yes, it is! It was my cousin's, but she thought it made her look washed out, so she passed it along to me," Caro told her.

Yes, Caro had changed, all right, Emily thought. A few weeks ago, she would have *died* rather than confess that any of her beautiful, expensive clothes were hand-me-downs!

The rest of the Fillies, who had been watching the meeting between Caro and Eric as though it were a scene from a television soap opera, clustered around Emily's parents, giving them a warm welcome—all except Dru. She was still lying face down on her bunk, and the only indication that she knew they were there was a little wave of one hand.

"Emily dear, what's wrong with Dru?" Mrs. Jordan murmured in Emily's ear. "Is she ill?"

"No, she's okay. Or at least, she's not sick or anything," Emily said. "She's just feeling sad again, because she's afraid her folks aren't going to show up. She thinks they've forgotten all about her."

"Oh, dear! The poor thing!" Emily's mother glanced over at Dru with real concern. She knew all about Dru's situation from Emily's letters. "Hasn't either of them written or phoned?"

"No—Dru hasn't heard from them since last week. That's why she's so upset."

"I'm not surprised," Mrs. Jordan said. "Do Matt and Marie know?"

Emily shrugged. "I'm not sure. Probably not. I don't think Dru would have told them, and none of us have said anything."

"Well, I will! And, in the meantime, let's try to make Dru forget about her troubles."

Mrs. Jordan marched over and sat down on the edge of Dru's bunk, resting a hand gently on her shoulder. Before she could say anything, Dru jerked away. "Just leave me alone, okay? My stomach hurts. I think maybe I'm going to be sick . . . ."

"I'm not surprised that your stomach hurts," Mrs. Jordan said. "But I don't think you're going to be sick. I bet you're hungry, that's all. And you know something? So am I!"

At the sound of her voice, Dru lifted her head and stared at her. "Mrs. Jordan! I didn't know it was you!"

Just then, everybody heard the clang of the dinner bell calling the campers to their evening meal.

"See? What did I tell you? It's time for supper, and I don't know about you, but *I* am *starving*," Emily's mother said cheerfully. "I'm surprised you can't hear my stomach rumbling. But I think I can hear yours! What say we hurry up to the farmhouse before the Thoros and the Foals eat up all that good fried chicken Marie told me she's prepared?"

"Yes, Dru, get a move on," Emily added, smiling at the younger girl. "We have to eat fast so we can come back here and change for the moonlight trail ride."

Mr. Jordan and the rest of the Fillies were already on their way—all except for Caro, who was deep in conversation with Eric.

"You *are* coming on the trail ride with us, aren't you?" she asked. "Like I told you in my last letter, it's all right with Matt and Marie. And you can ride the same horse you rode when you were here last time."

Eric grinned. "I've been looking forward to it."

"So have I!" Caro purred, fluttering her lashes.

Still completely absorbed in each other, they wandered out of the cabin, and Emily, her mother, and Dru followed. On the way to the farmhouse, Mrs. Jordan put an arm around each of the girls, asking countless questions about what they'd been doing since Emily's last letter. Emily let Dru do most of the answering, and, by the time they entered the dining room, Dru seemed a lot happier. Mr. Jordan had saved places for all of them, and he paid special attention to Dru all through the delicious meal. Emily didn't mind at all—she was glad to see a smile on Dru's face. And she thought, not for the first time, how lucky she and Eric were to have such really super parents.

Later that evening, after Mr. and Mrs. Jordan had left to check in to their room at the Riverside Motel, the Fillies, the Thoros, and Eric set off on their moonlight ride. It wasn't quite dark yet, but the moon was already visible in the twilight sky. Pam, on Firefly, her big, rangy bay gelding, was in the lead, and Chris, riding his horse, Buster, brought up the rear. There was a chill in the air, a reminder that summer was almost over and autumn was on its way. High overhead, a flock of barn swallows circled and whirled in their graceful evening dance.

"I wonder why they do that every night?" Libby mused aloud as she rode next to Emily along the riverbank.

"Maybe they're comparing notes about everything they've done during the day and everywhere they've been," Emily replied dreamily. "Or maybe it's just their way of saying good night to us." She paused. "Or good-bye."

"Or maybe they're really lovebirds," Libby said with a giggle, "and they're sending a message to *those* two lovebirds on horseback!"

Emily knew exactly what she meant. Caro and Eric were riding side by side ahead of them, gazing into each other's eyes. She still couldn't quite get used to her big brother acting so goofy over a girl. She hadn't gotten used to the fact that he was growing a moustache, either, but she guessed she would in time. *Growing a moustache—growing up.* Emily shivered a little, though it wasn't really all that cold. To change the subject, she said, "Where's Dru?"

"She and Penny are right in front of Eric and Caro," Libby told her. "She's okay now, I think, thanks to your folks. But if her mom and dad don't show up, I don't know what she's going to do. Some parents she's got!"

Emily sighed. "I know. Mom said she was going to tell Matt and Marie that they might not come, and if they don't, I guess it's up to the Websters to decide what to do with her. Poor Dru!"

"Yeah—poor Dru," Libby echoed. "And it's not fair, because she's a really nice kid. If they *do* come at the last minute, I'd like to—well, I'd like to tell them just exactly what I think of them!"

"But you won't," Emily said.

Now Libby sighed. "No, I guess I won't. But I can sure give them some awful dirty looks!"

Chapter Nine

Very early the next morning before the other Fillies were awake, Emily got up and dressed, pulling on a bulky sweater over her Webster's T-shirt. Then, she took an apple and a popcorn ball wrapped in wax paper from the little shelf over her bunk and tiptoed out the door. The popcorn ball was left over from the ones the Foals had made while the older campers were on the trail ride last night, and Emily had saved it as a special treat for Joker on her next to last day at Webster's.

It was cold outside—really cold, not just chilly. Emily could see her breath as she hurried across the dew-damp grass, and her wool sweater felt nice and warm. As she approached the pasture where the horses spent the night, Emily could see Joker grazing next to Pepper, Penny's little sorrel. The morning sun began to warm the earth, and a low ground mist was making all the horses look as though they were knee-deep in clouds. Emily paused for a moment, taking in the dream-like scene and engraving it on her memory. It was a mind picture that she knew would stay with her for a long, long time, far sharper and clearer than any video could possibly be because it was hers alone.

She whistled now, and Joker, recognizing the sound as her special signal to him, raised his head and began ambling over to the fence. He greeted her with a friendly whicker, perking up his ears and stretching out his neck in anticipation of the treat he knew she'd brought him.

"Oh, Joker," Emily sighed as she gave him a hug, "I wish you were really and truly my very own horse! Then, when I go home tomorrow I could take you with me." The palomino butted his head gently against her chest, then began snuffling around the pockets of her jeans. Emily laughed. "All right—I get the picture. You don't really love *me*. It's the goodies you're after." She took the apple out of one pocket and held it out on the palm of her hand, stroking Joker's neck as he took it and started to munch. "Come to think of it," she told him, "if you *were* my horse, we'd have to rent a trailer for you or something. We couldn't very well squeeze you into the back seat of the car between Eric and me! And you probably wouldn't like living in our garage next to Dad's car." Joker snorted and shook himself all over, and Emily giggled. "I didn't think so. Here— have a popcorn ball. Oops—wait a minute so I can take the wax paper off."

Joker wasn't too sure about the popcorn ball, but after a cautious snuffle or two he gobbled it right up. "Sticky, isn't it?" Emily said. "And I guess it isn't

very good for your teeth, but since this is my next to last day here . . ." Suddenly she felt all choked up. Blinking back the tears that stung her eyes, she put her arms around his silky, golden neck, resting her cheek against him. "I'm going to miss you something awful," she whispered.

"Hey, Emily, that you?" Chris Webster came running across the pasture toward her, surrounded by swirls of mist.

Emily quickly wiped her eyes with the back of her hand and sniffed. "Hi, Chris," she said in what she hoped was her normal voice. "What're you doing here so early?"

"Dad wanted me to take the horses to the stable before breakfast because parents will start arriving pretty soon and he'll need me to help show them where to park and where to find their kids," Chris told her. "Warren was supposed to meet me here, but he's probably still asleep—his rock band played a gig last night, and he got home pretty late. Want to give me a hand?"

Emily nodded. "Sure. What do I do?"

"Just hang out while I open the gate and make sure they all follow me, then close the gate behind us." Chris went over to Buster, led him to the fence, clambered up, and sprang onto Buster's bare back.

"Uh . . . what if they don't?" Emily asked nervously. "Follow you, I mean. What if one of them starts to run away or something?"

"Don't worry about it. We do this every morning and no horse has ever run away yet," Chris assured her. "Besides, they know there's oats and hay waiting for them in their stalls. Horses aren't dumb, you know."

"I certainly do!" Emily exclaimed. "Joker's smarter than some *people* I've met." She watched as Chris rode over to the gate, leaned down, expertly unlatched it, and swung it open. Holding Joker's halter, she waited while the rest of the horses and ponies obediently filed out of the pasture behind Buster, their hooves making hardly any sound on the lush green turf. She knew every single one of them by name, and who they'd been assigned to for the summer. Lynda's dapple gray Dandy, Dru's plump little Donna, Dark Victory, Pepper, Foxy, Danny's mare Misty, Firefly, Queenie, Pogo, Cupcake, Led Zeppelin, Socks, Mr. Bill, Lucky, Midnight . . . and of course, the most beautiful one of all, Joker.

Closing the gate behind them, Emily suddenly remembered the words of a lullaby her mother used to sing to her when she was very little:

"Hushabye, don't you cry,
Go to sleep, little baby.
When you wake, you will see
All the pretty little horses.
Red and gray, black and bay,
All the pretty little horses . . ."

Humming softly to herself, she led the big palomino toward the stable.

*　　　*　　　*

Eric, who had slept over at the farmhouse, joined the Fillies for breakfast. Mr. and Mrs. Jordan planned to come back to the camp around noon, in time for the picnic lunch Marie had planned for the campers and their families. It would be the first official event of Parents' Weekend, though not all the parents would have arrived by then.

After breakfast, Matt went over the schedule of activities for the next two days. "I know this is an exciting time for all of you," he began when everybody had quieted down, "and it is for me and my family, too. We're looking forward to meeting those parents we haven't met before, and to renewing acquaintances with the others—like Mr. and Mrs. Jordan, and Eric, of course." He smiled at Emily and Eric. "But we still have our chores to do, so this morning's routine will be pretty much as usual. When a camper's family arrives, we'll welcome them and tell them where their daughter can be found. Your parents can watch your riding classes if they get here in time, and then, as you know, everybody is invited to a picnic up in the grove. During rest period, feel free to show your families around the camp, introduce them to your horses, whatever. Everybody is welcome to participate in water sports, and after that, we're going to have a showing of the video Warren's been taping for the last few days. It won't be edited, of course, but I know you'll enjoy seeing yourselves in action. . . . What is it, Laura?" he asked, turning to the little girl, who was bouncing up and down in her chair at the Foals' table, waving her hand wildly.

"You didn't tell them about the brand-new, super-huge TV my daddy bought for the camp," she said excitedly. "It just got delivered yesterday afternoon and it's in the Activity Room so there's lots of room for lots of people to watch it! Isn't that neat?"

Matt nodded solemnly. "It certainly is, and I was just about to mention it, but you beat me to it."

"Well, I just wanted to make sure you didn't forget," Laura chirped.

Matt grinned at her. "Thank you, Laura." Addressing the rest of the campers, he went on, "Next on the agenda is supper, to which all families are cordially invited, and then this evening is . . ."

"Parents' Night," Libby called out. "Only in my case, it's Grandparents' Night!"

"Right you are, Libby. And Marie and I were kind of hoping that your grandmother might bring her friend along to take part in the show."

Libby looked puzzled. "Her friend?" Then she understood. "Oh, you mean Madame Beatrice, the gypsy fortune-teller! You know, she just might!"

All the campers clapped and cheered—"Madame Beatrice" had been a big hit a few weeks ago at the campfire. Emily still wasn't sure how she managed to tell the campers' fortunes so accurately, and Libby was forced to admit that she wasn't, either.

Matt tapped on a glass with his knife, and the chatter died down. "Tomorrow, as you all know, is the last horse show of the season. It will take place in the morning, and afterward we'll have a barbecue." He paused. "And after that comes the part

Marie and I *don't* like about Parents' Weekend. That's when you girls who have been members of our family all summer are reclaimed by your *real* families and go back home."

"Not all of us," Dru mumbled sorrowfully. *"Some* of us might be here *forever!"*

"Don't be silly, Dru," Emily whispered. "That's not going to happen and you know it!"

Dru just sighed.

"What's the matter with her?" Eric asked Caro.

"I'll tell you later," Caro whispered. "Matt's going to say something sentimental, and I think I'm going to cry!"

"I just want to tell every one of you that we care about you very much," Matt said gruffly, putting his arm around Marie, who had come over to stand beside him.

"Matt's right—we love having you here, and we're going to be very sad when you leave. You wouldn't believe how lonely it is with only us Websters around the place!" she said.

Caro began to sniffle, and Eric picked up a paper napkin and handed it to her, looking concerned. Emily's eyes were teary, too, but Eric didn't offer *her* a napkin. Lynda, however, said loudly, "You and all the horses!" and everyone laughed.

"Right, Lynda—us and all the horses," Matt said, smiling at her. "But they're going to miss you, too, and like the rest of us, they'll be looking forward to your return next summer, when Webster's will be bigger and better than ever."

"That's because of Daddy," Laura piped up

proudly. "He's going to build a swimming pool, and some new cabins, and a lodge, and . . ."

"Yes, indeed!" Marie cut her off. "And we're all going to have a wonderful time."

Libby leaned over and whispered to Emily, "I just hope they don't change the name of the camp to Frick's!"

Emily couldn't help grinning. "If Laura has anything to say about it, they will—*Laura* Frick's Country Horse Camp!"

All the Fillies giggled, even Dru.

" 'Scuse me, Dad, but Mr. and Mrs. Davidson are here," Chris said, sticking his head in the dining-room doorway. Beth leaped up from the Thoros' table, and Matt nodded his permission for her to leave and greet her parents.

"Well, so much for emotional speeches," he said as Beth headed for the door. "The season's not over yet, and I know you're all eager to get your horses groomed so they'll look their best when your families arrive. Marie and I will see you at the picnic."

"And, by the way," Marie added, "kitchen detail is hereby suspended for today and tomorrow." When her announcement was met with applause and cheers, she laughed. "Guess that's one thing you *won't* miss about Webster's, right? The counselors are going to help with meals, and I have some people coming from town to give us a hand. And Mrs. Jordan has volunteered as well, so I promise there'll be plenty for everybody to eat. But the Thoros are still on breakfast cleanup, so I'd appreciate it if they cleared the tables."

"Jennifer Richards, your folks just drove up," Chris hollered from the doorway.

Jennifer grabbed Laura's hand. "C'mon! I can't wait for you to meet my mom and dad!" she cried as the two girls ran out of the room.

"Coming, Dru?" Penny asked, pausing by her friend's chair.

"Why should I? Nobody's coming to see me *or* my horse." Dru remained slumped in her seat.

"Oh, yeah? Well, if that's what you think, you're wrong," Libby said. "There's my grandpa, for instance."

"Why would your grandpa want to see me?" Dru asked without much interest.

"Because he only saw you dressed up as the Wicked Witch in the Costume Parade at Field Day, and he didn't believe Gram and me when we told him you were really a very pretty, normal-looking girl. In the last letter I got from them, Grandpa said, 'Be sure to tell that little witch that I'm looking forward to seeing if she's as pretty as Gram says.'"

Dru brightened a little. "He did? He really said that?"

Libby looked her straight in the eye. "Would I lie to you?"

"Well, in that case . . ." Dru got up. "Okay, Penny, I'm coming."

After Penny and Dru had left, Emily turned to Libby. "*Did* he really say that?"

With a twinkle, Libby said, "Well, if he didn't, he *should* have!"

Emily grinned. "You're right. And considering

how much better it made Dru feel, let's just assume that he did." Then she became serious. "But if Dru's folks don't show, it's going to take more than your family or mine to *keep* her feeling better!"

Chapter Ten

By the time riding classes were over and everyone had gathered in the picnic grove for lunch, most of the campers' mothers and fathers, along with the occasional sister, brother, uncle, or aunt, had arrived. Emily met Penny's parents, and Danny's. Mr. and Mrs. Marshall were both short, stocky, and fair-haired like Penny, but though Mr. Franciscus was dark and exotic looking, like Danny, Mrs. Franciscus was slender, willowy, and pale.

The big surprise was Caro's parents. Emily had expected them to look like the couples she'd seen in magazines advertising imported cars or designer clothes, but Mr. and Mrs. Lescaux weren't like that at all. Mr. Lescaux was a big, beefy man with a receding hairline and a great, booming laugh, and Caro's mother, in a madras wraparound skirt, navy blue polo shirt, and horn-rimmed glasses, reminded Emily very much of her favorite English teacher back home. She felt completely comfortable with them both, and she could tell Eric did, too. Mrs. Lescaux immediately asked Marie if she could help serve the food, and soon she, Marie, and Emily's mother were chatting away like old friends while Mr. Lescaux, Mr. Jordan, and Eric consumed vast quantities of potato salad and roast beef sandwiches as they talked about Eric's favorite topic, cars.

During the picnic, Matt and Mr. Frick circulated among their guests as Matt introduced his new partner. Laura dragged her mother over to meet Emily and Libby, her two "big sisters." Mrs. Frick turned out to be a small, round woman with a sweet face. She didn't have much to say for herself, which wasn't surprising since Laura, as usual, did all the talking. After Mrs. Frick had trailed off in Laura's wake, Emily said to Libby, "Do you think your grandparents will get here in time for the show tonight? It would really be terrific if 'Madame Beatrice' did her fortune-telling routine."

"Who knows?" Libby replied cheerfully. "Gram and Grandpa don't stick to any timetable. I've learned to expect them when I see them, but they never, ever let me down . . ." She glanced over at Dru, who was standing with Penny and Mr. and Mrs. Marshall, nibbling on a carrot stick and looking sad. ". . . unlike *some* people's relatives I could mention!"

For the rest of the afternoon, the grounds of Webster's swarmed with happy campers and their families. All the Fillies' parents made a special effort to include Dru in whatever they did, but Emily thought her gloomy presence was like a small rain cloud in an otherwise sunny sky. She cheered up a

108

little when everyone gathered in the Activity Room to see the video, and Lynda stuck with her back in the bunkhouse afterward as the rest of the Fillies' mothers and fathers helped them get a head start on packing their belongings.

"I don't see why I have to pack," Dru said mournfully, sitting on the edge of her bunk and staring at her open camp trunk. "I'm not going anywhere. I'll probably still be right here when you all come back next summer."

"For Pete's sake, Dru!" Lynda sighed. "You act like you're the only girl at Webster's whose family hasn't arrived yet." She groped under Dru's bunk and pulled out one sock. "Is this clean or dirty?"

"Dirty, I guess. You can stick it in my laundry bag."

"Gee, thanks!" Lynda teased. "I get all the fun jobs."

Mrs. Jordan sat down beside Dru, putting an arm around her shoulders. "I know how you must feel, Dru, but believe me, everything's going to be all right. Emily's father and I have spoken to Matt and Marie, and if your parents don't arrive in time for the horse show tomorrow, they'll make inquiries. But I'm sure they *will* turn up. Who knows—they might even make it to Parents' Night. Wouldn't that be a nice surprise?"

"It'd be a surprise, all right," Dru mumbled. "Thanks, Mrs. Jordan, for trying to cheer me up. I'm sorry to be such a . . ."

"Wet blanket?" Libby suggested.

"Yeah, something like that." Dru smiled a little. "I'll try not to be."

"Good!" Lynda said briskly. "The only blanket we need in our act tonight is the one you, Penny, and Caro will be under when we do 'Daisy, Daisy'!"

Eric, who had been waiting patiently while Mrs. Lescaux helped Caro fold and pack Caro's dozens of dresses, skirts, blouses, and shorts, said to her, "You're going to be under a blanket? What kind of act is it, anyway?"

Caro made a face. "You'll have to wait and see, just like everybody else. And remember, when you do, I'll be the one in *front*!"

"Drat! My moustache keeps falling off," Danny complained later that evening as the Fillies prepared to perform their barbershop routine. Through the partly opened door to the Activity Room they could hear the Thoros doing their skit, to the accompaniment of laughter from the appreciative audience. The Foals and Laura, all in costume for their part of the program, were clustered around the door, peering through the crack to see what was going on while Melinda did her best to keep them quiet.

"Use some more chewing gum," Libby said. "Has anybody seen my straw hat?"

"This shirt is *way* too big," Caro muttered. "I think Pam must have given me one of Matt's!"

Emily looked at her and grinned. In her baggy shirt, straw hat, and fake moustache, Caro looked just as silly as the rest of them did. "You know,

Caro," she said, trying to keep a straight face, "you and Eric are the only couple I've ever heard of where the *girl* has a bigger moustache than the guy!"

Melinda moved away from the door and whispered, "They're almost done, Fillies. Are you all set?"

They all nodded. Then suddenly Penny hissed, "The horse! Where's the horse?"

"He's right over there, on that chair," Lynda told her. "Melinda's going to help you, Dru, and Caro put him on when the time comes. You okay, Dru?"

Dru smiled. "I'm fine. I won't foul up, I promise."

Loud laughter and applause signaled the end of the Thoros' skit, and Melinda took up her post by the door again, watching while they took their places in the audience so they could see the rest of the show. When everything had quieted down, she cleared a path through the excited Foals so the Fillies could make their entrance. "You're on, gang," she said softly. "Break a leg!" Seeing Dru's startled expression, she added quickly, "That's just another way of saying 'good luck.'"

For a moment, Emily panicked. Her mind went completely blank—she couldn't remember a single word to any of the songs, not even the ones she'd written herself.

"*Move,* Emily!" Libby whispered, giving her a little poke.

Emily moved, and discovered that, as soon as she and her cabinmates took their positions, everything she was sure she'd forgotten came flooding back. From then on, she simply relaxed and had fun. The

audience loved their act, particularly "Daisy, Daisy"—the dancing six-legged horse was such a hit that they had to do the number again, and when Caro, Penny, and Dru came out from under the blanket as the Fillies took their bows, Emily could hear Eric's and Mr. Lescaux's laughter above all the rest.

Delighted with their triumph, the Fillies found seats wherever they could to watch the Foals perform. The baton twirler didn't drop her baton once and Jennifer's tap dance was bright and perky, but the star of the show was definitely Laura Frick as the bounciest Peter Rabbit ever. Emily clapped with genuine enthusiasm, and Libby, who was squeezed next to her on the same folding chair, shouted, "That's our little sister!"

When the applause finally died down, Emily expected that Matt would turn on the lights and invite everybody into the dining room for refreshments. He stood up, but instead of turning on the lights, he said loudly, "Ladies, gentlemen, Thoros, Fillies, and Foals! We have a special treat for you tonight—a return engagement, by popular demand, of that world-famous gypsy fortune-teller, Madame Beatrice!"

Libby let out a little squeal. "She made it! She's here!"

A small figure dressed in brightly colored garments and glittering with golden bracelets, necklaces, and huge hoop earrings entered the room and strode to the center of the stage area. In her hands she held what looked like a crystal ball, though

Emily knew it was only a big, round light bulb. But this time, "Madame Beatrice" must have hooked it up to some batteries or something, Emily decided, because it seemed to glow with a dim, pulsing light.

The gypsy gazed out over the audience, and said in a thick accent, "I am Madame Beatrice, mind reader and fortune-teller! I tell you ze past, ze present, and ze future!" She raised her crystal ball, peering intently at it. "Ze past! Yesterday . . ."

Before she could say any more, the campers all shouted, "Vas Friday!"

Madame Beatrice grinned. "Ze present . . ."

"Iss Zaturday!"

"And ze future . . ."

"Vill be Zunday!"

"You know vhat? You're right!" The gypsy lowered the crystal ball. "Now I tell fortunes. Who vants to be first? Don't be shy—*you!*" She pointed directly at Eric, who was sitting with Mr. and Mrs. Jordan near the front. Grinning sheepishly, Eric edged down the row and came up beside her.

Emily clapped her hands over her mouth to stifle a giggle. "This ought to be good!" she murmured to Libby.

"Giff me your hand," Madame Beatrice commanded. "I read ze palms, too—ze crystal ball is not always reliable vhen ze batteries are running low." She shifted the ball to one hand and took Eric's with the other. "Aha! You haff come long vay to see a girl . . . no, *two* girls! Vone of zem iss a relatiff—a zizter, maybe?"

"How does she know that?" Emily gasped.

114

"You got me," Libby said. "Listen."

"And ze ozzer iss . . ." The gypsy bent over Eric's hand, looking at it closely. "Ze ozzer iss . . . *not* your zizter!" Everybody laughed. "Ze ozzer girl . . . can ziss be? Ze ozzer girl hass ze head of a *horse!*"

This time the laughter was even louder. *She must have seen our act,* Emily decided.

"Ze girl wis ze head of a horse iss very beautiful and very nice," the gypsy went on. "You make her happy, and she makes you happy. You are lucky boy."

Blushing, Eric stumbled back to his seat as the audience clapped and laughed. Madame Beatrice read many other palms and told many other fortunes. Then she looked out into the audience and pointed at Dru.

"Me?" Dru squeaked.

"You," said the gypsy.

When Dru stood beside her, the gypsy didn't ask to see her hand. Instead, she peered into the crystal ball.

"I guess the batteries aren't as worn out as Gram thought," Emily whispered to Libby. "It's glowing like anything."

Madame Beatrice's voice was very soft as she said, "You are not a happy girl. But that will not last. The thing you fear will not happen, and your dearest wish will come true."

Emily noticed that the gypsy's accent seemed to have disappeared. She sounded very much like Libby's Gram.

"My dearest wish?" Dru repeated. "You mean . . ."

"I mean vhat I say." The accent had come back, and Madame Beatrice patted Dru's cheek. "You vill find out tomorrow. And now, I sink it iss time ve all had zome of Marie's vonderful refreshments!"

Red, yellow, and blue pennants fluttered merrily against a bright blue sky the following morning as the final horse show of the season began. The bleachers around the Advanced riding ring were crowded with spectators. Music blared from Chris's tape player, and Joker, his golden coat gleaming in the sunlight, pawed the ground impatiently as Emily, in her best riding clothes, stroked his glossy neck.

"Easy boy," she crooned. "You'll have to wait a while—the Beginners' competition comes first, then us."

Caro came up next to her on Dark Victory. She was grinning from ear to ear. "Look at your crazy brother!" she giggled, pointing to where Eric was seated with Emily's parents. Mr. and Mrs. Lescaux and Libby's grandparents sat beside them.

Emily looked and grinned, too. Eric had fastened Caro's black handlebar moustache to his upper lip and, when he caught Caro's eye, pretended to twirl one end of it like an old-fashioned villain. "I have to admit it looks better on him than it did on you!"

Now Matt entered the ring and the Beginning riders, Laura and Dru among them, gathered at the gate. The show was about to begin.

116

As Danny rode Misty over to join Caro and Emily, she pointed across the field and said, "Whoever those people are, they'd better hurry or they're going to miss the first class."

A couple was walking hand in hand across the grass. The man was tall and thin, and the woman's pretty face looked anxious. Suddenly Dru caught sight of them, and her face lit up just the way the gypsy's crystal ball had the night before. She dug her heels into Donna's plump sides, urging the little mare into a trot.

"Mom! Dad! You're *here*!" she cried as she approached them. "You didn't forget about me!"

Emily, Caro, and Danny looked at each other, and all three faces reflected Dru's joy and relief.

"About time," Libby muttered, coming over to join them on Foxy. But she was smiling, too.

Dru slid out of Donna's saddle and flung her arms around her mother, then hugged her father. "I was so *worried*!"

"Oh, honey, we're sorry," Mrs. Carpenter said, embracing Dru again. "But we had to visit your sisters' camp, and then the car broke down somewhere around Albany. We tried to phone several times, but the lines were always busy . . . . Dru, baby, you look *wonderful*!"

"You sure do," Mr. Carpenter added. "You're so much slimmer, and I think you've grown, too."

"Dru, come on! Our class is starting," Laura called out.

"Be there in a minute," Dru called back. Then she gazed from her mother's face to her father's.

117

"There's just one thing I'd like to know," she said. Her expression was very solemn now. "I'm awfully glad you've come to take me home, but what I want to know is, *which* home? Who am I going to be living with from now on?"

Mr. Carpenter put his arm around her and said gently, "You're coming home with both of us, baby."

"Yes, but where am I going to *live*?" Dru asked anxiously. "With Mom or with you?"

"We only have one home, Dru," her mother said, smiling. "Your father and I have done a lot of talking and thinking over the summer, and we decided that our separation was a very bad idea. We love each other and you children too much to split up. We still have some things to work out, but we're a family, honey, and that's the way we're going to stay."

"Oh, wow!" was all Dru could say as all three of them hugged each other again. When she had dried her happy tears, she said, "The gypsy was right. My dearest wish came true!"

Mr. and Mrs. Carpenter looked puzzled. "The gypsy?" Dru's father echoed.

"Never mind. I'll tell you all about it later." Donna had been placidly grazing nearby, and now Dru gathered up her reins and swung up into the saddle. Beaming down at her parents, she said, "Wait till you see what a good rider I am! You're going to be proud of me."

Mr. Carpenter put his arm around his wife's waist. "Honey, I have news for you. We already are!"

As Dru, followed by her parents, trotted off to the ring, Emily blinked away her own happy tears. "What do you know about that!" she sighed.

Turning to Libby, Caro said, "What *I* want to know is, how did *Gram* know about that?"

Libby shrugged. "I don't think she did, not really. But she's a pretty good guesser sometimes."

"I'll say she is!" Danny said. "Let's go watch Dru's class, okay?"

Libby and Caro rode along with her to the fence surrounding the ring, but Emily stayed behind. "I'm so glad everything worked out for Dru," she told Joker softly. "It's been a wonderful summer—the most wonderful summer of my entire life! And you're the most wonderful horse—but you know that, because I tell you every single day. I'm really going to miss you—but you know that, too . . . ."

"Hey, Emily, aren't you going to watch the show?" asked Chris, coming up beside her on Buster.

"Yes, in a minute. I was just talking to Joker," Emily said a little sadly. "I'm starting to miss him already!"

"Uh . . . Emily, I was wondering . . ." Chris's voice trailed off.

"What?"

"Well, I know how nuts you are about that horse and everything, and I thought—well, maybe I could write to you sometimes, tell you how he's doing and stuff like that. You wouldn't have to write back or anything if you didn't want to . . . . Oh, forget it! I guess it was kind of a dumb idea."

"Oh, Chris, it's *not* a dumb idea!" Emily cried. "It's a super idea! And I *will* write back, honest I will."

Chris grinned. "Okay. I'll read your letters to Joker so he doesn't forget who you are."

They began riding side by side toward the ring. "And next summer, Judy and I will be here together," Emily said, her eyes shining. "And so will Libby and Caro and Lynda and Danny and Penny and Dru . . . . Gosh, Chris, I can hardly wait! It's only ten months away!"

ABOUT THE AUTHOR

Virginia Vail is a pseudonym of the author of over a dozen young adult novels, most recently the ANIMAL INN series. She is the mother of two grown children, both of whom are animal lovers, and lives in Forest Hills, New York with one fat gray cat. Many years ago, Virginia Vail fell in love with a beautiful palomino named Joker. She always wanted to put him in a book. Now she has.